Summer
of
Secrets

Rosie Rushton lives in Northampton. She is a governor of the local Church of England secondary school, a licensed lay minister and passionate about all issues relating to young people. Her hobbies include learning Swahili, travelling, going to the theatre, reading, walking, being juvenile with her grandchildren and playing hopscotch when no one is looking. Her ambitions are to write the novel that has been pounding in her brain for years but never quite made it to the keyboard, to visit China, learn to sing in tune, and do anything else God has in mind for her, with a broad grin and a spring in her step. Her many books for Piccadilly Press include *Tell Me I'm OK, Really; Friends, Enemies and Other Tiny Problems; Secrets of Love* and several series including *Best Friends; The Leehampton Quartet* and *What a Week*.

Summer of Secrets

ROSIE
RUSHTON

Piccadilly Press • London

First published in Great Britain in 2007
by Piccadilly Press Ltd,
5 Castle Road, London NW1 8PR
www.piccadillypress.co.uk

A catalogue record for this book is available from the
British Library

ISBN: 978 1 85340 907 3 (trade paperback)

1 3 5 7 9 10 8 6 4 2

Printed and bound in Great Britain by Bookmarque Ltd
Cover illustration by Susan Hellard
Cover design by Fielding Design
Text design by Carolyn Griffiths, Cambridge
Set in Goudy and Caslon

This book is dedicated to Colin and Mary Wake, who apart from being as enthusiastic about the writings of Jane Austen as I am, have walked the walk with me over many years and to whom I am very deeply indebted.

My thanks to Kate Little for her invaluable help on the flora and fauna of Liguria – not to mention her snippets of local colour!

To Unity College students Jack, Paige, Louise, Joseph, Jenna and Darryl, for their valued input and to Joan Mackness for making it happen.

To my fantastic editor, Ruth Williams, for always hitting just the right note.

And to all those wonderful SAS members (Scattered Authors Society, not Special Air Services!) who cheered me, encouraged me, put up with my whinging and generally shared their amazing pool of talent with me. Thank you.

✤ CHAPTER 1 ✤

'No one would have supposed her born to be a heroine ...'
(Jane Austen, *Northanger Abbey*)

'SO CAN I? CAN I COME OVER TO YOUR PLACE ON SATURDAY?'
Izzy Thorpe pranced over to Caitlin, who was sprawled
on one of the beanbags in the Day Den and gazed down
at her with sea-green eyes as wistful as if she'd been some
poor, homeless kid longing for a bed for the night,
instead of the daughter of a cabinet minister and a
woman whose knitwear designs were sought after by the
glitterati of the world.

'To my place?' Caitlin asked, looking up reluctantly
from her new copy of *Goss* magazine and raising her
voice above the babble of Year Eleven students crashing
in for morning break. It wasn't that she didn't want to
spend time with Izzy – in fact, she couldn't wait to build
on this new friendship. It was just that she'd rather do it
anywhere other than in her own home. She had spent
the past three weeks trying to create the right image here
at Mulberry Court and she wasn't about to blow it now.

Getting the Hector Oliver Art Scholarship was just

the start, she knew it was: the gateway to the sort of life she had always known she was destined to lead. In the three weeks she'd been on the induction programme for the following term's Sixth Form intake, she'd realised that to make friends with these guys would be her passport to better things.

'Caitlin!' Izzy prodded her in the ribs impatiently. 'So is it a deal? I can't wait to meet your family!'

'Why?' Caitlin thought it was a perfectly reasonable question, given the nature of her nearest and dearest.

'*Why?*' echoed Summer Tilney, brushing past her and grabbing a paper cup from the stack by the water cooler. 'Use your head. She's been gagging to get to your place for days.'

Caitlin sighed inwardly and tossed her magazine to one side, resigned to having to wait to discover the identity of the secret love of reality-show star Lisa Loretta. Clearly, Izzy had no idea what it was like to share a ramshackle house with four brothers and sisters, two dogs, a variety of cats, gerbils, mice and chickens and a couple of parents who had clearly been absent when anything approaching style or finesse was being handed out. Her father earned shed loads of money, she was sure of that; but he was so busy saving for what he called a 'rainy day' that none of it got spent on anything remotely relevant to an upmarket lifestyle.

Compared with everyone else she'd met at MC, her life was without doubt the most boring and unsophisticated. Summer, who played three instruments and sang like an angel, was the daughter of the marmalade magnate, Sir Magnus Tilney; Isabella's dad was an MP and he and her mum were in and out of the news on a monthly basis; and Bianca Joseph's mum was an ageing rock diva with her own Lear jet and houses in three continents. Even the kids whose parents weren't so high profile seemed to live fascinating lives in which every weekend was spent sussing out the latest clubs or dashing between divorced parents and ripping off both sides for new clothes and the latest MP3 players.

Which made it all the more unfair that someone like her – someone with passion and sensitivity and a deep connectedness to the finer things of life – should be afflicted with a family who could win Oscars for dullness. Sometimes she wondered whether her mother, who was, after all, absent-minded at the best of times, had picked the wrong baby from the maternity ward and that in reality, Caitlin was from a family oozing with class and eccentricity and a total dedication to the pursuit of glamour and excitement.

Caitlin, much as she adored her parents, had to admit that they were not big on excitement. Her father was the sort of man who in the olden days would have been called 'worthy'. Edward Morland, in addition to being senior partner in the highly-respected law firm of Morland, Croft and Isingworth, sat on numerous charitable committees, campaigned in favour of traffic calming in the high street and against litter universally, drove old ladies to church (often when they didn't even want to go) and, on the rare occasions when he did something for himself, played chess. Not just on the infrequent evening when there was nothing worth watching on TV, but for the local club and even for something called Chess42morrow, which sounded trendy but actually was all about teaching innocent little kids to learn the game and grow up to be as boring as he was.

As for her mother, Lynne Morland was the original earth-mother type: having finally given up reproducing after the unexpected arrival of child number five, she spent her time baking bread, growing organic vegetables in their garden in Ditchcombe (runner up in the Prettiest Village in Sussex competition for three years running), masterminding the local flower show and avoiding any activity that could possibly drag her into the twenty-first century. Caitlin loved her to bits, but there was no way she was about to parade her and her unfortunate dress sense in front of her new friends – especially when those friends had parents who knew how to live life to the full.

'Caitlin!' Izzy prodded her in the ribs. 'You're day-dreaming again. So I'm coming, right? I so want to sort out my party and we could do it together at yours.'

'But we all said we'd meet up in Brighton on Saturday night – and besides, we could do the party stuff at your place,' Caitlin reasoned. According to Summer, Izzy's parents were totally laid back and didn't give a toss what their kids got up to – whereas her lot could sniff out a hidden bottle of vodka a mile away and would have no shame about marching into her room at half-hourly intervals to check that she wasn't doing anything vaguely imaginative or interesting. They didn't treat her brother like that, of course, because—

'It's Jamie, isn't it?' Caitlin burst out, as the reason for Izzy's persistence finally registered in her wandering brain. '*He's* the reason you want to come over – go on, admit it.'

Izzy flushed and avoided Caitlin's gaze.

'Don't be silly – of course it's not,' she began. 'Why – will Jamie be around this weekend?'

Caitlin sighed. What it was about her brother she didn't know, but despite showing no interest in them at all, he managed to have girls prostrating themselves at his feet, whereas the story of her own love life would fill the back of a postage stamp with room to spare.

'*Will* he?' Izzy couldn't hide the eagerness in her voice.

Caitlin shrugged.

'Haven't a clue,' she replied. 'He's a law unto himself. But I guess if I tell him you're coming . . .'

'No way! Don't you dare!' Izzy screamed. 'I so don't want him to think that I—'

'Fancy him like crazy?' Summer interrupted, gulping down the last of her water and tossing the cup into the bin. 'Or was that yesterday? We all know that you fall in and out of love more often than the rest of us touch up our lip-gloss.'

'I do not! And besides, do you *have* to reduce every emotion to the lowest common denominator?' Izzy retorted, pulling a face at Summer. 'I don't *fancy* him – that is such adolescent terminology.'

Summer shook her head, raised a perfectly arched eyebrow, but said nothing.

'I just think he's a really interesting guy,' Izzy finished lamely, surveying a broken fingernail with distaste.

'When Izzy says a guy is interesting,' Summer whispered in Caitlin's ear, 'it means two things. One, she's got the hots for him and two, she's about to make mincemeat of him. When she has this party of hers just make sure you don't let *your* boyfriend anywhere near her, OK?'

Caitlin smiled what she hoped was an enigmatic smile and turned to gather up her magazines and grab her text books. She wasn't about to admit that she didn't have a boyfriend, or even a friend who was a boy right now. If she had been glamorous like Izzy, who, with flawless skin and hair the colour of liquorice, looked like a gypsy princess out of some Offenbach operetta, or dainty like Summer – whose skin was so pale that it seemed transparent and who reminded Caitlin of that poem about fairies with gossamer wings – she might have had more luck on the guy front. But she was what her mother called 'chunky', had auburn hair that fought her hair straighteners every morning and won, and such a healthy, freckled complexion that no one believed she was ill, even when she felt at death's door.

Despite these drawbacks, however, she was basically an optimist and she was pinning all her hopes on next term. Mulberry Court, a rambling grey-stone building nestling in a cleft of the South Downs in Sussex and advertised as 'the Country's Foremost Independent School Specialising in Expressive Arts', had started taking boys in the Sixth Form and she hoped that she could do some hands-on expressing with the two she'd got in her sights – Fergus Walker and Charlie Ditton. She had earmarked the summer holiday for losing weight, getting lowlights and becoming sophisticated; and she thought that in addition perhaps she would ask Izzy's advice about getting boys to come on to her. Certainly, Izzy's techniques seemed to be working on Jamie.

She sighed to herself, recalling that first morning three weeks earlier when Jamie had agreed to drop her off at school – not through any sense of brotherly love and duty, but because he'd just returned from three months in Australia and wanted to give his battered MG Midget a burn-up. Caitlin had been battling to open the passenger door – Jamie hadn't got round to fixing anything that wasn't under the bonnet – when Izzy appeared at her elbow.

'Hi, I'm Izzy,' she had said brightly, her eyes fixed, not on Caitlin, but very firmly on Jamie's bronzed thighs, shown off to considerable advantage by his frayed denim shorts. 'Caitlin and me are best buddies.'

This statement had somewhat surprised Caitlin, since she'd only met Izzy at the scholarship interview day, during which, although she was supposed to be showing Caitlin the ropes, she'd spent more time buffing her nails and sizing up the guys in the Sixth Form than forming any lasting relationships with the newcomer.

Jamie, who was usually more given to grunts than whole sentences, had treated her to a lopsided grin, said 'Hi, Izzy, good to know you,' and then thrown the gear stick and roared off, his macho departure being only slightly spoiled by the necessity of stopping after ten metres to avoid a double-decker bus.

'*Where*,' Izzy had gasped, grabbing Caitlin by the wrist, 'did you find him? That is one seriously divine guy.'

'Divine? Jamie? Be serious,' Caitlin had said, laughing.

'You mean – he's not your boyfriend?' Izzy had asked.

'No way,' Caitlin had replied. 'He's my brother.'

'Oh my God!' Izzy had clamped a perfectly manicured hand to her mouth, slipped her arm through Caitlin's and begun dragging her towards the imposing entrance of Mulberry Court. 'What are you going to think of me? I mean, I thought he was your guy and I was just trying to – well, you know – be friendly and stuff.'

She had kicked open the double doors.

'Lovely necklace, by the way,' she had remarked, gesturing at Caitlin's pendant. 'I wish I had more junky stuff – all mine's *real*, and wearing it here would be so in your face, know what I mean? OK, now this is the Day Den – or common room, to the rest of the world. Shove your stuff over there. By the way, your brother – has he got a regular girlfriend?'

Caitlin had shaken her head.

'Nobody serious – he spends most of his time messing around with cars,' she had sighed. 'Why?'

'Oh – no reason,' Izzy had assured her. 'Just showing an interest.'

Izzy had continued to show an interest at regular intervals ever since, which was quite clearly, Caitlin thought, as she stuffed her magazines into her bag, why she was so keen to come over on Saturday. More surprisingly, Jamie appeared to have noticed her friend as well; he had insisted on driving Caitlin to school several times in the past couple of weeks, albeit on the excuse that the car needed some fine tuning; he had gone through the 'Ciao, Izzy – see ya around!' stage, to the 'How's your mate Izzy? She seems kinda cool,' stage every evening, and the previous day he'd actually winked at Izzy as he drove off, which, while not being the greatest come-on by some people's standards, was as good as a declaration of intent for Caitlin's reticent brother. And clearly, Izzy had got the message and had decided it was time to go in for the kill.

'So that's settled,' Izzy gabbled, as the bell rang. 'I'll pitch up on Saturday – we can still make Brighton for the evening – we'll sort out the party and get Jamie to come along with a few of his mates and—'

'Jamie? You're going to ask him to your party?' Caitlin gasped.

'And you tried to pretend you don't fancy him?' added Summer.

Izzy gave them both a long-suffering stare.

'I'm doing it for *Caitlin*,' she said graciously. 'She doesn't know many people, and having Jamie there will make it easier for her. What's the matter? Why are you laughing?'

'And what strikes you about this picture?'

Robina Cathcart, the new history of art tutor, zapped

the button on her laptop and *The Three Graces* filled the screen on the studio wall.

'Serious cellulite!' Izzy called out, pointing at the three naked ladies of more than ample proportions. The entire room collapsed in fits of giggles. Izzy made no secret of the fact that art was not her thing; she was the school's drama queen in more ways than one.

'That is not funny,' Mrs Cathcart said, her huge jade earrings tinkling as she shook her head impatiently, causing wisps of bottle-blond hair to escape from her chignon.

'No, you're quite right, Mrs Cathcart – cellulite is certainly no laughing matter,' Bianca Joseph added with mock solemnity.

'As, indeed, she should know,' whispered Izzy, nudging Caitlin in the ribs.

'Is there anyone in this room who can think of a single intelligent thing to say about Rubens's work?' Mrs Cathcart demanded. 'How about our new art scholar? Caitlin?'

'Me?' Caitlin looked alarmed. This was only her second lesson in history of art, and she was feeling distinctly out of her depth. The practical stuff, such as photography, painting, doing caricatures of her mates – all of that came easily to her; but when it came to comparing and contrasting the work of Monet and Van Gogh, or identifying a fragment of an Italian fresco, she was lost. Everyone else in the room, it seemed, had toured the art galleries of Europe or thought nothing of owning the odd Constable or Whistler. Her parents' idea of a family holiday was a cottage on the Isle of Wight and all that bedecked the walls of Caitlin's home were ceramic plates and framed photographs of the Morland children at every stage of their development.

'Yes, you,' the tutor encouraged. 'Tell us what you see.'

Caitlin swallowed hard.

'Well,' she began, peering more closely at the picture, 'obviously the woman in the middle is really having a hard time of it – I guess she's being bullied by the other two. They're pretending to be oh-so-nice, of course, but you can see they are really laying into her – criticising her figure and all that. See how they are gripping her arms, not letting her get away. I guess probably she's used her magical powers as a goddess or whatever to win the affection of some nobleman that they're after and that's why . . .'

She stopped dead. Half the class had swivelled round in their seats and were eyeing her with a mixture of astonishment and outright hilarity.

'All right, Caitlin, you've had your joke,' Mrs Cathcart said wearily. 'Now would you please give us the facts about the picture. When was it painted?'

'Um – quite a long time ago?' Caitlin ventured.

'For heaven's sake, girl – how come we gave you a scholarship?'

Caitlin felt a dozen pairs of eyes fixed on her, waiting for her next *faux pas*. Get this wrong, and she'd be labelled an ineffectual wimp and the cool set would be closed to her for ever. Even Summer, who normally kept her eyes down and worked like a swot, seemed to be egging her on to say something more incriminating.

'I guess because I'm pretty ace at drawing; because my photographic portfolio was wacky and off the wall and because when I'm a top designer, it won't matter a toss whether I know when some stupid man obsessed with fat women was born!'

For a moment you could have heard a pin drop. Mrs Cathcart's ample breasts heaved in unison, her poppy red lips pursed together and Caitlin just knew that she had totally blown it. She'd be expelled before she'd even started and then her family would be able to smile in satisfaction and say it was all for the best and she should have kept her feet firmly on the ground.

'All right, point taken!' Mrs Cathcart smiled despite herself. 'You're right – well, up to a point, anyway. You *do* have tremendous artistic talent, and there'll be plenty of opportunities for me to drum some of the finer points of art history into you. A task which will clearly take some time. In fact – you've given me an idea.'

A groan rippled round the room.

'Her ideas always mean hard work for us,' said Izzy. 'Thanks a bunch, Caitlin.'

'An assignment,' Mrs Cathcart began.

'You can't – it's practically the end of term!' Bianca protested.

'We'd never have time to do it justice,' Izzy added emphatically.

'It's a holiday assignment,' Mrs Cathcart replied smugly. 'I'm calling it *Art in My Imagination* and . . .'

'We don't *have* holiday assignments,' Summer burst out. 'When we had Mr Brington, he never gave us anything to do after the end of term.'

'Did he not? Well, I do,' said Mrs Cathcart, smiling calmly. 'As I was saying, I want you all to seek out one piece of art wherever you go on holiday this summer and let it speak to you – the way Caitlin, however misguidedly, let *The Three Graces* fire her imagination. Paint, draw, photograph anything and everything that the original painting or sculpture leads you to think about. Make up stories, poems . . .'

She beamed round the room, clearly chuffed at her own inventiveness.

'And then I want you to find out where the artist *really* got his inspiration – myths, legends, unrequited passion – and compare the two. Should be fascinating.'

'Oh, riveting,' muttered Bianca, as Mrs Cathcart turned away and packed up her laptop. 'Like she really thinks I'm going to find a load of art galleries in the Maldives. Get real.'

The Isle of Wight isn't exactly spilling over with masterpieces either, Caitlin thought.

'I'll expect a portfolio from each of you at the start of next term,' Mrs Cathcart concluded. 'Good morning, ladies!'

'I shan't know where to begin,' Caitlin moaned as she made her way to lunch with Bianca, Summer and Izzy. 'I've never done anything like this before.'

'It could be quite fun,' Summer mused.

'*It could be quite fun*,' Bianca imitated. 'Compared to what? Watching paint dry?'

'Compared to spending the whole holiday . . . oh, forget it!'

'Go on,' Caitlin urged.

'I said, forget it!' Summer turned away and stomped over to the food counter.

'Is she OK, do you think?' Caitlin asked anxiously, watching as Summer grabbed a tuna salad. Falling out with one of the few friends she'd made would not be a good idea right now, and secretly she thought Summer fascinatingly mysterious.

'She'll be fine,' Izzy replied confidently. 'She's like that – starts to tell you something and then clams up like she's hiding a state secret. I guess it's – well, you know, what with her father and everything.'

'What about him?' Caitlin asked eagerly.

'Well, there's a rumour going round that he's got – hang on, she'll hear us,' Izzy muttered, and then raised her voice as they caught up with Summer. 'Hey, how about we hit the shops after school? You up for it, Summer?'

Summer shook her head.

'No thanks,' she replied. 'Ludo's got tickets for a jazz concert – sorry.'

She pushed past them and headed for a table in the far corner of the dining hall.

'Who's Ludo – her boyfriend?' Caitlin asked.

'Boyfriend? Summer? Hardly!' Izzy retorted, grabbing a cheese and tomato roll. 'If you ask me, there's something seriously not right with her.'

'What do you mean, not right?'

'She's not into boys,' stressed Izzy. 'Or at least, in the whole two years she's been at Mulberry, I've never seen her with one. Is that odd or what?'

'You mean, she's . . .' Caitlin hesitated, not quite sure how to put it.

'I'm not saying *that*,' Izzy said. 'But she never drools over fit guys in magazines and she's not very sociable – I mean, she never throws a party or has anyone back to her place or anything. She's a real loner. She won't even commit to coming out with us lot on Saturday night.'

'So who's this Ludo?' Caitlin looked suspiciously at what passed for lasagne, before taking a jacket potato and a scoopful of coleslaw and heading over to Summer's table.

'Her brother,' Izzy said with a shrug. 'She's got two – Freddie, who's dead cool and Ludo, who isn't. They're twins, although you'd never know it. Apparently they've both been bumming round Europe on a gap year, lucky sods.'

'Hardly bumming in Ludo's case!' Summer looked up as they reached her table, apparently recovered from her fleeting fit of pique. 'Freddie's the bumming expert – most of the time Ludo's been at Casa Vernazza, learning the ropes.'

'Casa what?' asked Caitlin.

'Oh – it's our house in Italy,' Summer replied, nibbling on a black olive. 'We've got this vineyard in Begasti – it's near Monterosso and it used to belong to my grandparents. Freddie's not remotely interested, so Dad's got it into his head that Ludo will take it over one day.'

'You own a vineyard? That is so amazing!' Caitlin

gasped, anxious to restore normal relations. 'Just like that movie – what's it called? *Under the Tuscan Sun.*'

'It sounds a lot grander than it is – it hardly makes any money at the moment. It is lovely, though – well, it was until . . . Hey, is that the time? I've got to dash – piano lesson.'

With that she pushed her half-eaten salad to one side and almost ran out of the room.

'She is *so* lucky,' breathed Caitlin. 'Just imagine living in Italy, surrounded by all that history and art and romance.'

'Like I said, Summer doesn't do romance,' said Izzy. 'Talking of which . . . what time shall I come to yours on Saturday?'

🜲 CHAPTER 2 🜲

'Something must and will happen to throw a hero in her way.'
(Jane Austen, *Northanger Abbey*)

'OH MY GOD, IS THIS YOUR BEDROOM? I'VE NEVER SEEN anything like it.'

Izzy flopped down on Caitlin's bed and gazed at the sand-textured walls, midnight blue canopy over the bed and the candle sconces on the wall.

'Do you like it?' Caitlin asked eagerly. 'I did it all myself. Needless to say, the parents can't stand it.'

She had been relieved to get Izzy upstairs at last, and out of the clutches of her mother who from the minute Izzy arrived had been plying her with questions, food and instructions in equal measure.

'So, Isabella, dear, your mother does know you're here, doesn't she? I know what you young people are like for dashing off . . .'

'Now, dear, a little carrot cake? Homemade, of course, and all organic and GM free . . .'

'Isabella, dear, I wouldn't sit there if I were you – the cat was sick on the cushion this morning and I haven't got round to washing it . . .'

At that, Caitlin had grabbed her friend by the wrist and dragged her up the stairs, cringing inwardly at what she was sure Izzy must be thinking. Although Caitlin had not as yet been inside Izzy's house, driving past it had been enough to give an idea of the lifestyle to which her friend was accustomed – it was an elegant, three-storey Regency town house, overlooking the seafront at Brighton, with ironwork balconies and bow windows and a general air of being a property just waiting to feature in some lavish period movie. Whereas the Old Parsonage would have been the ideal choice for one of those make-over programmes that have architects and designers throwing up their hands in horror at the enormity of the task before them. To Caitlin's artistic sensibilities, it was an embarrassment – a mish-mash of uncoordinated colours and styles, every room cluttered with objects that her mother assured her she could never part with even though they appeared to have no practical or aesthetic use whatsoever.

'This is all a bit – well, Addams Family, isn't it?' Izzy queried doubtfully, eyeing the gargoyles stuck to the bedroom wall and black ceiling with coloured bulbs hanging in clusters.

'It's Gothic,' Caitlin explained enthusiastically. 'It goes with the view. See for yourself.'

Izzy jumped off the bed, walked over to the window and shrieked.

'Oh my God, Caitlin – that's so spooky! How can you sleep with all – well, *them* out there?'

She stared with a mixture of horror and fascination into the neighbouring churchyard, lined with yew trees and scattered with headstones in varying stages of decay.

'You get used to it,' Caitlin assured her. 'It's haunted, of course, but most of the time—'

'Haunted? You mean – you've actually seen a ghost?'

'Not *seen*, exactly,' Caitlin admitted reluctantly. 'More sort of *heard* them, and felt them. I'm a Scorpio you see and we're very intuitive—'

'And particularly talented at letting your imagination run away with you!' The door burst open and Caitlin's mum strode into the room, wearing bright orange rubber gloves with a none-too-clean apron covering her ample figure. 'Take no notice of her, Isabella dear—'

'Mum, I told you, she likes to be called Izzy,' Caitlin interrupted. 'And would you mind not eavesdropping on my conversations?'

'But Isabella is such a pretty name.' Mrs Morland sighed, ignoring her daughter's request. 'Listen, Jamie's just phoned – he's on his way back from that car auction. Thrilled about some spare part he's found apparently – and he's bringing a friend with him. Your father's going to attempt to barbecue—'

'Don't tell me Jamie's bringing a *girl* back!' Caitlin gasped in mock astonishment, more to wind Izzy up than because she actually thought it was even vaguely possible.

'He didn't go into the gender, dear,' Mrs Morland remarked dryly. 'But why shouldn't he? It would be nice to see him with a steady, sensible sort of girl.'

'That rules you out then,' Caitlin whispered to Izzy as

her mother left the room. 'So, come on, what about this party of yours?'

Although she was trying very hard to sound laid-back about the whole idea, Caitlin was pretty buzzed up at the thought of Izzy's seventeenth birthday. She couldn't believe how lucky she'd been, getting in so quickly with someone who was clearly the Queen Bee of her year; and even though she knew that it was, at least in part, only because Izzy saw her as a fast-track route to Jamie, she intended to milk it for all it was worth. Izzy was her passport to high society – and high society was where she knew she belonged.

'I don't know,' Izzy said. 'Last year I had a Bedouin and Belly Dancers, the year before that was Jungle Drums . . .'

'You mean, it's going to be fancy dress?'

'Sure – all my parties are. Only I'm running out of ideas.'

'Ghosts and ghoulies?' Caitlin suggested, rapidly trying to think of a costume that wouldn't cost her an arm and a leg to get hold of.

'Get a life,' Izzy retorted. 'I'm hardly going to look sexy wrapped in a sheet. I want to be alluring, smouldering, gorgeous . . . You do think Jamie'll come, don't you?'

'Not if it's fancy dress,' Caitlin had to admit. 'Getting him out of oil-stained jeans is hard enough. Trust me, I know.'

Izzy looked crestfallen.

'But he *has* to come . . . well, I mean, it doesn't really matter, but—'

Her final words were drowned beneath the sound of

scrunching gravel and squealing tyres in the lane behind the privet hedge at the bottom of the garden.

'What on earth . . . ?' Izzy flung open the window and peered out just as a stocky guy clambered out of a silver Mazda. 'Who the hell's that?'

At that moment, a second car, backfiring wildly, drew up by the gate.

'Well, that one's Jamie – you can tell by the noise. And you're safe. His mate's clearly a guy.'

Caitlin grinned at the look of relief on Izzy's face, a look which was followed by a dash across the room to Caitlin's huge pewter-framed mirror.

'Don't you dare mention the party!' Izzy insisted, flicking her hair behind her ears and peering critically at her flawless make-up. 'I'll kind of introduce the subject subtly when the moment is right.'

She paused, and turned to face Caitlin.

'That other guy he's with – does he look fit?'

Caitlin peered out of the window again as car doors slammed and the garden gate swung open.

'Average,' she reported. 'Arms too long, and he walks a bit like an orang-utan . . .'

'*Arms?* You are just the strangest person . . . what's his butt like? I go for backsides in a guy.'

'Can't see, he's gone out of sight,' Caitlin replied. 'Pretty cool car though. Anyway, I thought it was Jamie you're after.'

'I am not *after* him,' Izzy protested, glancing out of the window. 'I'm just . . . oh, never mind. Let's get down there – like, now.'

'*You?* What the hell are you doing here?' Izzy stood stock-still in the door of the kitchen, gawping at the stocky guy with sandy-coloured hair and a generous mouth who was leaning against the breakfast bar, picking from a bag of crisps.

'I don't believe it, it's Muffin!' the guy exclaimed in amazement.

'Don't call me that!' Izzy hissed, glaring at him.

The guy grinned from ear to ear and thumped Jamie on the arm.

'So this is your mystery girl!' he said and turned to face Izzy. 'He's been going on and on about this mate of Caitlin's—'

'Tom, shut it!' Jamie flushed scarlet and avoided Izzy's now-smug smile.

'Well, you don't have to worry about getting the inside track on her,' Tom said with a laugh, ignoring his embarrassment, 'because there's nothing you need to know about Izzy Thorpe that I can't tell you!'

'You don't know *anything* about me,' Izzy snapped.

'Come off it! I lived with you off and on for three years,' Tom replied. 'I've seen you drunk, throwing tantrums – and who gave you your first proper kiss?'

Izzy's face turned scarlet.

'Lived with . . . ?' Jamie began.

'Tom's my mum's godson,' Izzy explained, throwing Tom a look of pure disdain. 'His parents were overseas with the Foreign Office, and we got lumbered with him in the holidays because his mum and mine are old school friends.'

She turned to Jamie, her expression lightening.

'How come you know one another, anyway?'

'Gap year,' Jamie mumbled, viewing the floor tiles with some interest. 'Sailing in Australia.'

'Sailing? Oh, that is so my thing,' Izzy enthused.

This was news to Caitlin and judging by the disbelieving smirk on Tom's face, he wasn't convinced either.

'Anyway, don't listen to a word Tom says,' Izzy burbled on. 'He loves to wind people up. So, how was the car auction?'

'Ace!' Tom butted in before Jamie could reply. 'I bought a dream of a car – goes like the wind. OK, so the paintwork needs a bit of touching up and—'

'And the rest!' said Jamie, laughing. He opened the fridge and tossed a can of Pepsi at Tom. 'I still think you paid way over the odds – I mean, it's ten years old and you'll never get more than twenty-five to the gallon . . .'

'What's all this about a kiss?' Caitlin muttered to Izzy, as her brother and Tom embarked on a boring conversation about fuel consumption and carburettors.

'I was just a kid,' Izzy replied hastily. 'I only went along with it because I needed to improve my technique; he was on the spot, and had a car – it was before I developed any kind of good taste in men.'

Caitlin glanced at Tom, but although he had clearly overheard Izzy's remark, he seemed totally unfazed by it.

'I like to think I taught her all she knows,' he teased. 'Except how to change a tyre in the pouring rain.'

'Oh, you are so witty!' Izzy retorted sarcastically.

'Well, now, isn't that lovely?' Caitlin's mum, who had

caught the end of the conversation as she came into the kitchen clutching a bowl of strawberries, smiled happily at everyone. 'You're all getting to know one another.'

'And maybe you and I could get to know one another better!' Tom's words were the merest whisper in Caitlin's ear as he moved to shake Mrs Morland's hand, but there was no mistaking his hand on her bum. She glared at him, trying to ignore the little frisson of excitement that shot through her body, and stepped hastily to one side.

'The rest of the bunch are in the garden, so come along now,' Caitlin's mother ordered, waving through the window at Caitlin's father. 'Get those steaks on the barbecue, Edward!'

She bustled out through the back door and in one graceful move, Izzy was across the kitchen and smiling up at Jamie.

'So, your car – the one you drive Caitlin to school in – it's an MG Midget, isn't it? Round about 1978?'

'Seventy-nine,' Jamie replied. 'That's amazing! I've never known a girl who could . . . I mean, are you keen on cars?'

'*Passionate* about them!' Caitlin could have sworn that Izzy's eyelashes fluttered individually. 'Especially Midgets – the coolest cars ever. When I pass my test, that's the car I want. I'd die to go out in one.'

'I guess that could be arranged,' Jamie replied, smiling at Izzy.

It occurred to Caitlin that she'd never seen her brother hold anyone's gaze for so long.

* * *

{ 24 }

'You had this all planned, didn't you?' Caitlin demanded an hour later. '*Especially Midgets . . . I'd die to go out in one . . .* How subtle was that?'

'So? Don't you know *anything* about handling guys?' Izzy retorted, peering in the mirror as she applied a third layer of mascara. 'You have to find their weakness and then play it for all it's worth.'

'I thought,' Caitlin said petulantly, picking a remnant of corn on the cob from her front teeth, 'that you'd come to spend the day with me. Like, not.'

'Oh, come on, don't be like that,' Izzy pleaded, ramming her sunspecs on to the top of her head and grabbing her straw bag. 'It'll be fun! And it's not my fault Jamie's car only seats two. Anyway, I don't know what you're complaining about – you get to go with Tom.'

'But we're supposed to be meeting up with Bianca and Sophie later and—'

'We can still do that,' Izzy said. 'We'll drag the guys along too. It'll be cool.'

She looked beseechingly at Caitlin. 'You're not really miffed, are you? I think Tom's quite impressed by you, actually. Hey, wouldn't it be cool if you two got it together, and me and Jamie became an item and—'

'Hang on!' Caitlin objected, rummaging in her drawer for some sun block. 'I've only known the guy for an hour and besides, I'm not sure I even like him. *You* weren't exactly flattering about him.'

'That's because he isn't empathic to my persona,' Izzy declared. 'Whereas you, with your kind of naïve, unsophisticated approach to life . . .'

'Oh, thanks . . .'

'No, it's a compliment,' Izzy assured her. 'You're just Tom's type. I was far too fiery and ambitious and – well, full-on, I guess. Besides, we've known one another since we were snotty little kids, and that kind of kills passion, doesn't it?'

'I guess,' Caitlin said, nodding.

'He's OK, really. And the Porters are loaded, you know,' Izzy babbled on. 'I mean, *seriously* in the money. And they know just about everyone worth knowing.'

She winked at Caitlin.

'Besides, where's the harm? It's not like you've got a boyfriend, is it?'

'How do you know?' Caitlin burst out and then inwardly kicked herself for making it so obvious that Izzy was right.

'If you had, you'd have talked about him,' Izzy remarked. 'And think about it – my party's coming up and you don't really want to be the only girl there without a guy, do you?'

'You said Summer hasn't got a boyfriend,' Caitlin said quickly. 'It won't just be me.'

'Summer won't come,' Izzy said. 'I mean, I'll invite her, but she'll come up with some lame excuse. She always does. Mind you, if the rumours are true . . .'

'Yeah, what about the rumours? You were going to tell me—' Caitlin began.

'Hey, you two – we were actually thinking of leaving *today* if it's all the same to you!'

Jamie thumped on Caitlin's door and began to hum

'Why are we waiting?'

'Dead right – he needs to get started,' Tom added, shouting up the stairs. 'That old banger of his will take forever to get to the end of the street!'

'Is he always this up himself?' Caitlin demanded, picking up her camera and slinging it round her neck.

'Oh, loosen up!' Izzy snapped. 'Just look on him as a bit of practice. From what I can see, you sure do need it.'

Why, thought Caitlin to herself, as Tom threw the car round yet another bend at breakneck speed, can't I be like Izzy? There she was, ahead of them in Jamie's open-top Midget, her dark hair blowing out behind her like one of those shampoo adverts and her arm resting ever so lightly across the back of the driver's seat. Whereas Caitlin's hair was a mass of windswept tangles, she had grit in her left eye and she was already feeling nauseous, although whether this was caused by the recklessness of Tom's driving or the content of his conversation, she couldn't quite work out.

'That vehicle of your brother's is total crap, you know,' he told her. 'He really should take my advice and trade it in for something with a bit of power behind it.'

And, 'Honestly, if I hadn't pitched up at that sailing club in Cairns and shown him the ropes, your brother would have made a total ass of himself on the reef.'

And, just as she was about to open her mouth to defend Jamie, 'But sorry, I'm going on and on about Jamie when really I should be telling you about me.'

He was unreal, Caitlin thought, only half listening to

an outpouring about his triumphs on land and sea during his gap year, his reason for opting not to go to uni – 'Honestly, who needs it? It's *who* you know, not *what* you know that counts' – and his plans to take over his grandmother's chain of antique shops when she retired – 'Easy money – conning the Yanks into buying nineteenth-century tat.'

What clicked her concentration back on to full beam was the sound of Izzy's name.

'I hope Jamie's up to coping with Izzy – though somehow, I doubt it.' For the first time, there was a serious note to Tom's voice.

'What do you mean?'

'Oh, don't get me wrong – she's really hot stuff and great fun and all that – but not the kind of girl I would have thought Jamie would fall for. I mean, he's not exactly your way-out type and she's a bit on the wild side – know what I mean?'

'No, I don't really,' Caitlin admitted. 'I mean, I've only known her for a few weeks. And anyway, Jamie hasn't fallen for her, he's just being friendly . . .'

'Come off it – he's besotted!' Tom said, laughing. 'Talks about her all the time. Anyway, why are we wasting time talking about them? Tell me about you. What floats your boat?'

'Me?' Caitlin replied, wincing slightly as the nearside wheel of the car clipped a pothole at the edge of the road. 'Well, I like painting, photography—'

Her words were drowned by a sustained blast of Tom's car horn.

'Move it, JM!' he yelled, thumping the dashboard impatiently and tailgating Jamie's car. 'Foot on the accelerator, why don't you?'

'There's a speed camera down here,' Caitlin snapped, gripping the seat as Tom pulled into the fast lane and careered past the Midget. 'Slow down – you'll get zapped!'

'They're fakes,' Tom replied. 'Besides, I love playing traffic-camera roulette!'

He waved at Jamie in the driving mirror and turned to Caitlin, clearly no longer interested in talking about her.

'So, has Izzy planned her party yet?'

'You know about that?'

'Only that she's bound to be having one,' Tom said. 'She does every year at the start of the summer holidays. All the Thorpe parties are quite something – her parents have an amazing one every New Year. Last year's made it into *Harpers and Queen*.'

'Really?' Caitlin closed her eyes briefly, imagining herself, serene and stunning, smiling out of the pages of the country's most upmarket journal above a caption that read: *Society newcomer, Caitlin Morland, eclipsed all-comers at the party held in honour of Isabella Thorpe*—

Her reverie came to an abrupt end as Tom slammed on the brakes and screeched to a halt, threw the gear into reverse and backed hastily up the road on the hard shoulder, ignoring the rude gestures and blaring horns of other motorists.

'Missed the turn,' he said without a trace of remorse. 'Damn it – now Jamie's ahead of me and this road is useless for overtaking.'

Thank God for that, thought Caitlin.

'So where exactly are we going?' she asked, realising that no one had actually informed her of their destination.

'Barcombe Mills,' Tom replied. 'Izzy's idea – boating on the river. Her and Jamie, you and me – good, eh?'

He turned and grinned at her.

'Give you and me time to get to know one another a whole lot better, won't it? I mean – that's OK, isn't it?'

Since his eyes were fixed on her face, and there was a tractor and trailer crossing the lane a hundred metres ahead of them, and since for the first time that afternoon, he sounded just a little unsure, Caitlin nodded swiftly and sighed with relief as Tom turned his attention back to the road.

The guy was a bit of a pain, but he was a guy. And clearly he knew the right people. Maybe, just for a few weeks, he'd be an asset. Just to establish her as a goer in the eyes of her new friends – then she could shake him off. Just as soon as her reputation was well and truly established.

'So?' Izzy demanded, three hours later. 'Aren't you going to ask me?'

'Ask you what?' Caitlin sighed, turning the hot tap in the ladies' loo at the Boatyard Café.

'About me and Jamie!' Izzy pressed her eagerly. 'Go on, ask how we made out.'

'How did you make out?' she replied obediently.

'Brilliantly!' Izzy replied triumphantly. 'I mean, I

didn't let him know that, of course – I played it dead cool from start to finish . . .'

'Oh, sure – like I'm the Pope!' Caitlin said with a laugh, peering critically in the mirror at her sunburnt nose. 'Every time I saw you, you were positively salivating over him—'

'I so was not!' Izzy butted in. 'I'm not like that . . .'

'So when you stood up in the rowboat, shrieked and grasped his hand, and then held on to him for dear life for at least ten minutes . . .'

'You saw that?'

'I've got it on film,' teased Caitlin, tapping her camera case. '*Studies of a Serious Come-on* I shall call it!'

'It was only because my balance was affected by the bright sunlight,' Izzy said.

'Perhaps if you'd worn your sunspecs on your eyes rather than your head!'

'You,' said Izzy sighing, 'have a lot to learn. Anyway, what about you and Tom?'

Caitlin debated with herself for a moment before replying. If she told the truth – that the guy was so up himself that her strongest desire that afternoon had been to shove him headfirst into the weed-covered water and then photograph his slow demise – Izzy would spread the word that Caitlin Morland was a killjoy and no fun to have around. Besides, in between all the bravado, Tom had his serious moments – and those were quite endearing, in a surprising sort of way.

'OK,' she replied tentatively. 'I mean, it was fun – but I'm still not sure he's quite my type.'

'And what *is* your type exactly? You've never talked much about the guys in your life.'

That would take like all of two seconds, thought Caitlin. 'They have to have passion,' she began.

'Now you're talking,' Izzy said excitedly. 'Have you – well, you know. *Done* it?'

'Not that sort of passion!' Caitlin exploded, more from embarrassment than anger. 'I mean, depth and emotional intelligence . . . and no, I haven't – have you?'

'Not exactly,' Izzy admitted. 'But I live in hope. And I really think Jamie's the one – he's so divine . . .'

'You,' said Caitlin, blotting her lip-gloss with a tissue, 'are seriously in need of a sanity check.'

'But do you think he likes me?'

'Izzy, my brother has just agreed to come with us to Mango Monkey's, right? When there's the Grand Prix on Sky TV? Like, that's a really serious sacrifice in his book.'

Izzy hugged Caitlin.

'So, let's go! Oh, isn't being in love wonderful?'

'One apple and mango. Anything else?' The guy behind the bar at Mango Monkey's zapped the top off the bottle and slid it towards Caitlin.

'No, thanks,' she said, shoving a couple of pound coins at him. 'Keep the change.'

'Change?' he repeated in derisory tones. 'You need to give me another eighty pence.'

'That's a rip-off!' Caitlin exploded. 'It's only fruit juice.'

'I guess you pay for the monkey swizzle stick!'

Caitlin turned at the sound of a familiar voice, to see Summer Tilney clambering on to the neighbouring bar stool, wearing a gorgeous strappy pink sundress and looking decidedly jumpy.

'Summer! What are you doing here?' Caitlin gasped.

'Same as the rest of you, I guess,' she replied, gesturing across the room to where Izzy and Jamie were dancing and Bianca was chatting up two guys at the same time. 'Last Saturday of term, this is where we all hang out. It's tradition.'

'I know, but Izzy said that you never joined in – she said you hated clubbing and . . .'

'Despite what she may think to the contrary, Isabella Thorpe doesn't have the inside track on everyone,' Summer replied sharply, snapping her fingers at the barman. 'White wine and soda, please.'

'ID?' he queried, eyeing her suspiciously.

'Oh, stuff it, I'll have an orange juice,' she said. 'I keep forgetting this isn't Italy – over there I can drink Prosecco, Martini, whatever I like, and no one gives a toss.'

'It must be so lovely,' sighed Caitlin. 'What's it like – your house, I mean? Is it really romantic?'

'Romantic?' Summer frowned. 'How do you mean?'

'You know,' Caitlin urged, 'fountains in the gardens, frescoes on the walls, balconies overlooking cobbled courtyards . . .'

'You sound like you've swallowed a guide book,' teased Summer, breaking into a smile. 'It's lovely in a dilapidated sort of way – it's on a hillside below the vineyard, overlooking the sea.'

She smiled dreamily. 'You can walk through olive groves down to the beach or up the hill through the terraces to the castle. The village is all twisty alleyways and crooked little shops. When I was little I used to think heaven must look like Monterosso,' she said, laughing.

'It sounds amazing,' Caitlin breathed. 'And are you going there when term ends?'

'Yes – we—'

At that moment, Summer's mobile bleeped. She flipped open the cover, scanned the text message and then slammed it shut.

'Right, I'm off,' she said, sliding off the bar stool and grabbing her bag. 'See you Monday.'

'But you only just got here,' Caitlin protested.

'And now I'm leaving,' Summer replied calmly. 'It's a free country.'

'Hey, Summer – you made it!' Bianca, finally abandoning the two guys, sashayed up to the bar. 'This is like headline-making stuff – have you brought a guy? Or did you just come along to see Caitlin?'

Caitlin could tell from the way Bianca glanced over her shoulder at Izzy, who was clinging to Jamie's arm and heading their way, that this was a set-up job aimed at picking fun at Summer.

'Passion fruit and orange, please,' Bianca told the barman, and then turned to Caitlin. 'So where's Tom gone? You two were certainly going for it big time just now.'

'We were not,' Caitlin protested and then realised that she had swallowed the bait. 'Anyway, he saw one of his mates and he's disappeared somewhere.'

She glanced round the club and Summer followed her gaze.

'Oh no! Shit!' Summer gestured vaguely in the direction of the door, where a cluster of guys were about to enter the bar. 'I don't believe it. This is all I need. Look, if anyone asks, you haven't seen me, OK? I mean it. Both of you.'

She didn't wait for an answer but darted across the darkened dance floor and disappeared in the direction of the ladies' loo.

'See – even *talking* about guys terrifies her,' Izzy said, as Jamie tried to attract the barman's attention. 'You'd better watch out, Caitlin – I reckon she fancies you.'

'Get real,' Caitlin snapped. 'That is so not true. And anyway, what if she is – well, like that? It's no reason to make fun of her.'

'Pardon me for breathing,' said Izzy with a shrug. 'Hey, Jamie, come on – it's so hot in here. Let's go outside with our drinks. Coming, Bianca?'

Bianca shook her head.

'I've some serious pulling to do,' she replied, brushing her off with a gesture and turning to Caitlin.

'Now tell me, which one do you think?'

'Which what?' Caitlin mumbled, watching as Summer disappeared from view. She'd gone from looking calm and serene to acting like a terrified kid. What was going on?

'Which *guy*, silly,' Bianca sighed, jerking her head in

the direction of the two guys she had just abandoned. 'Simon – that's the dark-haired one with the earring, or Louis – he's French, and so smooth it's not true.'

'Go for him, then,' Caitlin told her. 'Definitely. The French are so romantic . . . Did you know that French guys have more testosterone than any other race? I read it in *Prego* magazine.'

'OK, so let's put the theory to the test,' said Bianca, laughing. 'You come over and keep Simon occupied, right? Bring the drinks, and I'll—'

'I'm not going to chat up a total stranger!' Caitlin protested.

'Adopt that philosophy and you'd never meet anyone,' Bianca retorted. 'Besides, what with Sophie getting sick and letting me down, I'm relying on you.'

She winked, flicked her hair over her shoulder and set off across the room, her eyes firmly on her unsuspecting prey.

Caitlin sighed, picked up the two glasses and began pushing her way through the snogging, dancing couples on the floor. There was nothing worse than sitting at the bar or wandering round the club trying to look as if she was about to join someone. And since there was still no sign of Tom, at least talking to this Simon guy would pass the time.

The room was getting more crowded and she was attempting to dodge the gyrations and waving arms of several couples who clearly thought they were preparing for the finals of *Strictly Come Dancing*, when someone knocked her arm.

'Hey, watch it!'

She spun round and gasped in horror at the sight of a large quantity of juice running down the cream chinos of a seriously fit-looking guy with the kind of suntan that definitely hadn't been acquired on Brighton beach.

'Oh gosh, sorry!' She dumped the empty glass on a nearby table, pulled a paper tissue from the pocket of her jeans, began dabbing at his thighs, realised what she was doing and stopped, cringing with embarrassment.

'Please, feel free!' the guy said with a lopsided smile. Caitlin felt her face flushing. He was gorgeous. Seriously, heart-stoppingly gorgeous. And she was a complete idiot.

'I'm sorry, really – I didn't mean . . .'

'Hey, it's no big deal! Let me get you another drink – something less likely to leave a stain this time? What'll it be?'

Caitlin stood staring at him, her mouth half open. He was at least twenty, she thought, with spiked hair that sported a sun-bleached streak down one side and the sort of slate-grey eyes you could drown in.

'Drink?' the guy repeated patiently.

'Oh – er, white wine and soda, please,' she replied with what she hoped was a dazzlingly confident smile. At least he looked old enough to get her a serious drink. 'And I'm sorry about the trousers.'

The guy shrugged. 'Forget it,' he replied, heading back towards the bar. 'Sorry – are you with someone?'

'No – well, yes – well, just mates, you know . . .'

She glanced across the club and was pleasantly

satisfied to see Bianca eyeing her in amazement.

'You're not one of Mulberry Court crowd are you?'

Caitlin nodded, wondering how he'd guessed.

'And I don't suppose by any lucky chance one of these "just mates" is Summer Tilney?'

Caitlin gasped and swallowed hard as Summer's words came back to her. *If anyone asks, you haven't seen me.*

'I haven't seen her,' Caitlin replied hurriedly. 'Not at all.'

'Ah, so you know her then?' the guy queried.

'Um, no – not really. I'm quite new, you see . . .'

Clearly this guy had unwelcome designs on Summer – had probably followed her with the express purpose of coming on to her. It must have been him who sent her the text; that's why she was in such a rush to go. Only last week, in *Prego* magazine, she'd read that cases of stalking were on the increase and that wealthy young society girls were prime prey. What with that, and Summer not liking men, she thought, she had to get rid of him as fast as she could. Which was a shame, considering he was such a babe.

'White wine and soda and a half of bitter, please,' the guy said to the barman, and then turned back to Caitlin. 'And you're quite sure— Sorry, I don't know your name.'

'Caitlin,' replied Caitlin, 'Caitlin Morland.'

'I'm Ludovic Tilney,' said the guy. 'But all my friends call me Ludo.'

'Ludo – Summer's brother?' gasped Caitlin.

'That's me,' he replied. 'So you *are* a mate of Summer's?'

Caitlin nodded. 'Yes, I'm on the induction course at Mulberry Court and Summer's been really nice to me.'

'Now, that *is* a recommendation,' Ludo smiled. 'Sum's going through one of her "I hate the entire universe" phases at the moment – the fact that she's spoken to you at all is rather remarkable.'

'Izzy said she was a bit of a loner,' Caitlin began. 'But the way I see it, there has to be a reason – there was this article in *Destiny* magazine that said that people who like their own company don't really *like* it at all, it's all down to their need to isolate themselves from any situation in which they could be challenged . . .'

She paused, realising that Ludo was frowning at her.

'I'm talking too much,' she apologised. 'I do that a lot. Sorry.'

She took a sip of her drink and frantically tried to think of something witty to say.

Out of the corner of her eye, she caught sight of Jamie and Izzy coming in to dance, clearly gobsmacked at the sight of Caitlin chatting up a guy.

'Well,' sighed Ludo, 'if Summer's not here, I'd better get going. I tried phoning but she won't pick up my calls.'

He gulped his drink down in one, his affable expression completely gone now.

'I don't suppose she said anything to you recently about meeting anyone – or stuff like that?' He sounded awkward and uptight.

Caitlin shook her head.

'Only if she did, I really need to know. I'm not being funny – it's for her own good.'

So that was it, she thought. Ludo knew about the stalker and realised that being the daughter of a millionaire industrialist put Summer at risk. He was just out to protect her from unsavoury fortune hunters.

'Well, to be honest—,' she began.

'So there you are!' Tom suddenly appeared at Caitlin's side. 'I've been looking for you everywhere.'

'I wasn't the one who went anywhere,' Caitlin replied pointedly, turning to Ludo. 'Actually, about Summer . . .'

Tom eyed Ludo suspiciously and then grabbed Caitlin's hand.

'Sorry, I was just chatting to an old mate of mine from the sailing club – I didn't mean to be so long.'

He squeezed her hand and looked apologetic. It occurred to Caitlin that he seemed a lot nicer when he was on the defensive.

'Come on, let's go on to *Funky Buddha's*. This place is too tame by half.'

He began dragging her towards the door that led out on to the seafront and then paused.

'Or would you rather go somewhere else?'

Despite her pleasure at being consulted for the first time that day, Caitlin wrenched her hand free and turned to Ludo.

'Please tell me where she is. This is urgent, believe me,' pleaded Ludo, completely ignoring Tom.

'She's here,' Caitlin burst out. 'I mean, now I know you're family, I can say. She's in the loo. See, she said that if anyone asked about her, I was to say I hadn't seen her, but I guess that was because . . .'

'OK, I get the picture.' Ludo said. 'Go and fish her out, will you? Please?'

'She won't like it,' Caitlin warned.

'Please – *I* can hardly go charging in there, can I? I'm doing it to save her skin, believe me.'

He smiled at her, head on one side and a pleading expression on his face. In that moment, Caitlin knew that she would have climbed Everest with Summer on her back if that was what he wanted.

'Why did you dash off like that? . . . made it so obvious. Now Dad . . . one of his rages . . .'

Caitlin averted her eyes from Tom's impatient, enquiring face and strained to hear the rather heated conversation that was going on outside the loos between Ludo and Summer.

'. . . it's just cruel . . . he has no right . . . immoral . . .' Summer's voice was brittle.

'. . . not fair on him, really . . . done his best . . . Can't you just humour him this once? '

'This *once*? Our whole lives are being turned upside down . . .'

Clearly something pretty serious was going on in Summer's life.

'. . . He's insisting . . . her birthday . . . You have to come now, Sum . . . You'll just have to face it . . .'

Suddenly, Summer's shoulders sagged; she picked up her bag and without a backward glance, followed her brother out of the door and on to the seafront outside.

Caitlin stared after them, the knots in her stomach

tightening as she recalled Summer's words to her in the loo.

'*And I thought you of all of them could be trusted to keep your mouth shut . . . How wrong could I be?*'

I've probably got her into deep trouble and she'll never speak to me again, thought Caitlin miserably, and if she doesn't, then there's no way I'll get to see Ludo again.

'OK, Izzy and me are heading off now.' Jamie came over to Caitlin, his car keys in his hand. 'Tom – you'll take Caitlin home, right?'

'Home? Already?' Tom asked.

Caitlin nodded. Now that Ludo had left, there suddenly seemed little point in hanging around anywhere.

'But first, Izzy and me just need the loo,' Caitlin said.

'No I don't . . .' Izzy began and then paused as Caitlin glared at her and nudged her in the ribs. 'On second thoughts . . .'

Caitlin shoved her through the door to the ladies'.

'About your party—' she began.

'Sorted,' Izzy interrupted. 'The theme's going to be a Night at the Movies. And what's more, you're wrong – Jamie's up for it!'

'It must be love!' Caitlin gasped.

'He said he'd go as Captain Jack from *Pirates of the Caribbean*,' Izzy said excitedly. 'I just know I'm not going to sleep a wink until I think of something . . .'

'Obvious,' replied Caitlin. 'You go as the Little Mermaid. Then he can rescue you from the billowing deep!'

'Oh, like I'm really going to wear a fishtail!'

'How about diaphanous blue chiffon with a skimpy thong underneath and little diamantes stuck on you to look like drops of water?'

'You're amazing!' Izzy cried in delight. 'That is so cool! Will you help me do it? *Pleeease* – pretty please?'

'On one condition,' Caitlin burst out eagerly. 'You have to invite Summer.'

'I said I would,' Izzy sighed, 'but she won't— oh my God! Don't tell me – I mean, you're not, you can't be . . .'

'You fancy her!' One of the cubicle doors swung open and Bianca, still zipping up her jeans, burst out. 'Tell me it's not true!'

'Oh, grow up, the pair of you,' Caitlin snapped, glaring at Bianca and turning back to Izzy. 'You've both got totally one-track minds. Just invite Summer to the party and make sure she brings Ludo. My whole life depends on it.'

'Ludo? Her brother?' Izzy gasped.

'Like how many Ludos are there in the world? *Of course* her brother – isn't he gorgeous?'

Izzy shrugged.

'So that was who you were talking to. I thought I recognised him – he's gone all blond. I guess he's OK, if you go for the head boy, butter-wouldn't-melt-in-my-mouth type, which I don't,' she said.

'So – it's *him* you want, not Summer?' Bianca asked.

'Of course it's him,' Caitlin sighed. 'Trouble is, I didn't have time to make any kind of impression – he was too uptight about finding Summer. Something about their dad being in a rage. What's all that about?'

'I don't think they get on that well,' Izzy remarked, reapplying her lip-gloss in the mirror. 'Summer and her dad, I mean. You see, ever since her mother died—'

'Her mum's dead? She never said.'

'Well, she wouldn't, would she?' Izzy added. 'Not under the circumstances . . . look, must dash – Jamie's waiting and I don't want him cooling off, OK?'

She winked at Caitlin.

'What circumstances?' Caitlin persisted, chasing after her as she headed for the door.

'Tell you later,' Izzy hissed. 'Right now, I've more important things to attend to. Like your brother.'

Three hours later, Caitlin was lying flat on her back in bed, staring at the fluorescent spider's web she had painted in the corner of her ceiling during a particularly bad dose of PMT. She was thinking about Ludo. She re-ran every detail of the evening, punching her pillow in fury each time she recalled her clumsiness with the drink, and then hugging it whenever she let her mind flash back to those slate-grey eyes and lopsided smile.

Tom had quizzed her like mad on the way home in the car, demanding to know who Ludo was, and saying that in his view he seemed a bit of a loser. And then he asked her to go to Izzy's party with him.

And like an idiot, she'd said yes, just to shut him up. But that didn't matter, did it? Once she was there, she could chat Ludo up and besides, going to a party with someone didn't mean anything, not really.

It was what happened when she *got* there that mattered to her.

It was no good; she couldn't sleep. She threw back the sheet and padded over to her drawing desk, grabbing a stick of charcoal and instantly sketching sweeping lines, her tongue poking out of the corner of her mouth the way it always did when she was engrossed in design. Within minutes, he was there: Ludo Tilney, smiling up at her from the sketchpad, his mouth slightly open as if he was about to speak.

Caitlin D Morland. Caitlin signed her name in the bottom right hand corner and then, in letters so tiny that no one, in the unlikely event of the picture being found, could possibly see them she added, *C 4 L* and the tiniest pink heart.

❧ CHAPTER 3 ❧

'If adventures will not befall a young lady in her own village, she must seek them abroad.'
(Jane Austen, *Northanger Abbey*)

'HEY, CAITLIN, WAIT!' SUMMER RAN DOWN THE STONE steps from the music block at breaktime on Monday morning and grabbed her friend's arm. 'I have to talk to you.'

Caitlin eyed her warily. Summer had ignored her totally at registration, hadn't spoken a word during music appreciation and she wasn't sure what was coming next.

'I was a cow on Saturday, OK?' she gabbled. 'You know, yelling at you and everything. Ludo told me he practically manhandled you to the door of the ladies' and forced you to find me.'

I wish, thought Caitlin. A bit of manhandling from Ludo would make my day.

'Everything had gone wrong and I was really stressed, but I shouldn't have taken it out on you.' Summer bit her lip and sighed. 'Friends?'

She opened her arms and looked pleadingly at Caitlin.

'Of course,' Caitlin replied, hugging her with relief. 'And so . . . is everything OK now?'

'On a scale of one to ten, it's about minus four,' she said wearily. 'But listen – what are you doing for the holidays?'

Caitlin wondered how to make a fortnight in the Isle of Wight sound stunning.

'Well,' she began, 'there's Izzy's party – and then my parents have taken a house on the island . . .'

That could mean anywhere, she reasoned. St Lucia, the Windward Isles . . .

'And you really have to go?' Summer looked crest-fallen.

'Well, I'm not likely to get a better offer . . .'

'That's where you are wrong!' Summer cried triumphantly. 'How does a couple of weeks with me at Casa Vernazza sound?'

Caitlin stared at her in disbelief.

'Me? You're inviting me to go to Italy with you?'

'Uh-huh,' said Summer, grinning. 'I just can't hack it on my own. Well, Ludo's coming, but he's always . . .'

What he was Caitlin didn't hear. She was too busy dealing with the images swamping her mind. Ludo and her swimming in the sea, his hand gently brushing her thigh under cover of the water; Ludo pouring a glass of cool wine and holding it to her lips; Ludo telling her how gorgeous she is . . .

'You don't want to come, right?' Summer's voice jolted her out of her reverie.

'*Of course* I want to come!' Caitlin exclaimed. 'I can't believe it – when do we go?'

'End of next week,' Summer said. 'It's only for two weeks because I'm going on a concert tour with the Music School but it would be so cool if you came.'

'And what about your dad?'

'What about him?'

'Well, I mean I couldn't help overhearing Ludo saying about his rages and . . .'

'Quite the little eavesdropper, aren't you?' Summer replied acerbically and then broke into a smile. 'Actually it was Dad's idea – one of his "sweetness and light" moments. He does have them occasionally – he's not all bad. Of course, I was about to say no way . . .'

'Why?'

'Because he's doing it to try to soften me up. "*It'll be a chance for Gabriella to get to know your friends . . . She's got heaps of fun ideas for you all*." Vomit making stuff like that.'

'Er – who's Gabriella?' asked Caitlin, although she was rapidly forming a pretty good idea of the answer.

'His new woman,' Summer muttered, through gritted teeth. 'Well, not new at all, really. She's been hanging around him like a lovesick puppy for ages. It's just that now he's decided to go public about her. And she's doing all she can to play the "future stepmother" bit.'

Her face clouded. 'I guess that was her plan all along,' she muttered. 'Pretending to be grief-stricken when Mum died and then sucking up to Dad . . . I hate her.'

She shook her head as if to rid her brain of these thoughts and her tone changed.

'Well, stuff that,' she went on. 'She's going to be there and there's nothing I can do about it, but if you come with me, it'll be more bearable. We can bum off any time we like. Tell them about the art project and say we're doing the galleries – there are loads of them – then we just go and have a good time. What do you think?'

'Sounds amazing,' breathed Caitlin. 'Thanks so much!'

'And your parents will be cool about it?'

Caitlin was not about to admit that 'cool' and her 'parents' were words that normally did not go together.

'Sure – no probs,' she assured her. 'None at all.'

'But we don't know these people,' Mrs Morland protested at supper that night, after Caitlin had poured out her plans. 'We can't let you go halfway round the world with just anybody.'

'Mum, it's Italy,' Jamie broke in, ladling more mashed potato on to his plate. 'Hardly the African bush. She'll be fine.'

Caitlin threw him a grateful look.

'When she goes, can I have her bedroom?' Anna, her thirteen-year-old sister asked.

'I'm going for two weeks, not for ever,' Caitlin told her. 'And you so much as set a foot inside my room—'

'This Summer Tilney – isn't she Magnus Tilney's daughter?' her father butted in. 'The marmalade people? I sat next to him once when he spoke at a Law Society dinner – seemed a decent enough chap as I recall.'

Caitlin reckoned that he didn't know the half of it,

but that this was not the time to set him straight. When he helped himself to more vegetables and winked at Caitlin, she was glad she'd kept her mouth shut.

'Can't see any problem with that,' he said with a smile.

'Hang on a minute, Edward,' her mother broke in. 'I'll want to meet them before I agree—'

'Great,' Caitlin interrupted hastily. 'I'll ask Summer over.'

'Not Summer, the parents,' her mother insisted.

'*Parent*, singular,' Caitlin remarked, putting on the most solemn expression she could muster. 'Her mother died under desperately tragic circumstances. That's why her dad wants me to go over there – to kind of cheer Summer up because she's still traumatised by it all.'

Just as she had hoped it would, this brought about something of a transformation in her mother.

'Poor lass,' she murmured. 'And how awful for the father. But a man on his own . . . no woman to keep an eye on the kids . . .'

'His new woman— er, there's going to be an aunt there,' Caitlin gabbled, remembering just in time her mother's view of cohabitation. 'And Summer said something about inviting other people too. *Please*, Mum . . .'

'Lynne, she's nearly seventeen,' her father remarked equably. 'It's time she spread her wings.'

'Yes, well, you would say that, you're a man,' said her mother. 'But she's very young for her years, and naïve and—'

'Well, I'm not going to get to grow up if you carry on

treating me like I'm still in nappies, am I?' snapped Caitlin. 'Besides, there's this art project we've got to do and Italy is just the best place on earth for me to guarantee getting an A star.'

'Well, I suppose in that case, it would be an experience.'

As Caitlin had hoped, the connection with schoolwork was clearly altering her mother's perspective. Her parents had not been at all keen on letting her go to Mulberry Court – which her father called an 'incubator for the moneyed classes' – but that didn't stop them wanting her to shine now she was there.

'You have to trust me, Mum – I'm not stupid,' she added hastily, for good measure.

Her mother smiled ruefully and nodded.

'You're right,' she sighed. 'OK, darling, you go and have a lovely time.'

'Mum, you're an angel!' Caitlin leaped up, nearly knocking over the water jug and hugged her mother.

'But there is one condition – we arrange to meet her father before you leave.'

'Yeah, yeah, whatever,' Caitlin said quickly. 'Oh, and just so you know – I'll be spending all day Friday at Izzy's house, helping her get ready for the party.'

'Oh yes – the party. I'm not comfortable about this,' her mother said. 'I've heard about these upper-class types snorting cocaine and all sorts. You *are* sure her parents will be there?'

'Of course they will.' Caitlin nodded, although she hadn't a clue where they'd be. 'And Jamie's going too.'

'Oh well, that's all right then,' her mother replied,

sounding relieved. 'Jamie's got his head screwed on the right way. I'm sure everything will be fine.'

'Sure it will. I mean, Izzy's dad's an MP, for heaven's sake – he's in charge of education. Izzy says he might be the next Home Secretary,' Caitlin added.

'Considering the state of this government,' remarked her father, 'I don't see that as any sort of recommendation.'

'Italy?' Even over the phone, Caitlin couldn't miss the astonishment in Izzy's voice. 'She's never asked anyone over for a *sleepover*, never mind a holiday.'

'Well, she said—'

'Not that I'd want to go,' Izzy raced on. 'Not with Summer and all her hang-ups. I wonder why she chose you? I've known her longer than you . . . Still, I'm sure you'll have a good time. '

'I know! It'll be so cool – but listen, you know you were saying about Summer's mum dying . . .'

'Oh, sugar!' Izzy butted in. 'My mother's yapping at the door, insisting I go to church with her. Honestly, my parents are such hypocrites – they hardly ever went till Pa got this cabinet post and now it's all this "we have to lead by example" stuff. Got to go!'

By the time term ended on Wednesday, Caitlin, to her great delight and surprise, was flavour of the month with at least half a dozen Year Elevens. Every time one of them got stressy with Izzy and said that this whole fancy-dress thing was too complicated and why couldn't she just have a normal hang-out type party with loads of booze and fit guys, Izzy sent them straight to Caitlin.

'She's a whizz with costumes,' she informed them all. 'She'll sort you. Of course, if you don't want to come . . .'

Since no one who valued their social standing for the following year would even consider falling out with Isabella Thorpe, Caitlin found herself inundated with requests for ideas.

'I have to look dazzling,' Bianca told her at breaktime on Tuesday. 'Now that Louis and me are a couple . . .'

'I didn't know things had gone that far!' Caitlin exclaimed. 'You only met him four days ago.'

'You've just been proved right,' Bianca said laughing. 'About the French and testosterone. He's one full-on guy. So, come on – what do I wear? Something that shows off my legs, since they're about my only asset.'

'Pocahontas,' Caitlin said decisively. 'You know, Native American – suede miniskirt, low-cut bodice, braided hair . . .'

'Kinky boots . . .!'

'I don't think they wore boots . . .'

'Well, they do now!' Bianca laughed. 'Neat – thanks, Caitlin.'

An hour later, it was Sophie's turn.

'I'm skint,' she told Caitlin, which for a Mulberry Court girl was quite an admission. 'I need something stunning but cheap.'

'Ann Darrow from *King Kong*,' said Caitlin firmly. 'See-through white nightie with spaghetti straps, gorilla handprint on one boob, hair loose . . .'

'Perfect!' Sophie cried. 'You convinced me as soon as you got to the see-through bit.'

'So, who are you going as?' Caitlin asked Summer later.

'Me? Oh, I'll think of something,' she said airily. 'It's no big deal.'

In between dashes to Brighton's North Laines market to get cheap fabric, sequins and ribbon; long sessions cutting, snipping and eating popcorn in her bedroom with a variety of mates; and a fair amount of time explaining to Jamie, as slowly and clearly as she could, that while cropped jeans with holes in could possibly be fitted into his costume, it was unlikely that a Pirate of the Caribbean would have *Silverstone 05* stickers as part of the ensemble, Caitlin worried incessantly about her own costume. She thought about the Ice Queen from Narnia, but dismissed that idea in case it suggested to Ludo that she was cold and frigid; she mulled over the idea of going as Hermione from the Harry Potter films but ruled that out as just too juvenile and goody-goody. She wanted romance tinged with tragedy; elegance with just a touch of the wild spirit . . .

'Oh my God!' The words escaped her lips even though there was no one in the room. 'That's it!'

The idea was stunning in its simplicity – but extreme in its daring. She grabbed her mobile phone and punched Izzy's number.

'Izzy? It's me. Listen, your party . . . what? Yes, your costume's ready – it's great. Come over and try it.'

She held the phone away from her ear while Izzy squealed in delight.

'Listen,' she went on hurriedly, 'I've had . . .'

No, she wouldn't say a word. Just in case Izzy told her she was way out of order. 'See you later, yes?'

She zapped the phone and flung it on the bed.

She couldn't believe she was going to do this, but then there was a lot happening in her life that she could hardly believe. Trip to Italy, party with one of the social elite, love affair with Ludovic Tilney . . .

Well, not a love affair yet. But if it didn't work out, it wasn't going to be for want of trying.

'About this trip to Italy – you said Summer's going to invite a whole crowd?' Jamie asked Caitlin early on the day of Izzy's party, while making a half-hearted attempt to remove oil stains from under his fingernails.

'Her dad's dead keen on the idea,' Caitlin said. 'Why?'

'Just wondered,' Jamie muttered. 'So – what's Izzy doing this summer?'

'You mean, you haven't asked her?' Caitlin teased. 'But then of course, what with your face being permanently buried in her neck, speech must be tricky and—'

'Shut it!' said Jamie, grinning. 'I was just wondering about her and me – well, you know – maybe, although of course she probably wouldn't want to, but it could be quite nice if . . .'

'You want to go on holiday with her, right? Snog her senseless in the sun?'

'Something like that, yes,' Jamie admitted, wiping his hands on a tea towel. 'Trouble is, I'm not exactly in funds right now – well, I've got a bit, but hardly enough for the five-star stuff she's probably used to . . .'

'Jamie, she adores you – she'd go anywhere to be with you.'

'Really? You think so?' Jamie looked as eager as a five-year-old let loose in a sweet shop. 'See, what I was thinking was, if you're going to be in Italy with Summer . . .'

'. . . that Mum and Dad might be cool about you two if they thought you were coming to Casa Vernazza as well?'

Jamie nodded. 'Do you think you can fix it?'

'I'll give it a go,' Caitlin promised. 'But Izzy said she wouldn't want to go to Italy with Summer.'

'That really means she desperately wants to, trust me,' Jamie said.

'For a guy, you're quite emotionally intelligent,' Caitlin conceded. 'And actually, another guy around might suit *my* plans rather well, too.'

Caitlin's heart pounded as she took a final look at herself in Izzy's bathroom mirror. She'd spent the whole of Friday helping to string fairy lights all round the huge basement of Izzy's house where the disco was set up, sticking movie posters on the walls and laying out food in the vast sitting room on the ground floor. Izzy was so lucky – Caitlin couldn't help wondering how her own mother would have reacted to having the house taken over; but Mrs Thorpe had simply told them to enjoy themselves and hurried off to join her husband at some Gala Ball at the Royal Pavilion, wearing what Caitlin was absolutely sure was a Versace gown.

'So what are you exactly?' Bianca queried as Caitlin emerged from the bathroom.

'Rose from *Titanic*, of course,' said Caitlin with a smile, tugging slightly at the bodice of her simple white dress (one that had started out in life as a pair of voile curtains) to show her cleavage to better advantage.

'Oh, yeah. Right.' Bianca sounded less than impressed but Caitlin didn't care. Her moment would come. 'Come on, let's hit the action.'

Two hours later, she wasn't feeling nearly so upbeat. Sure, she hadn't stopped dancing – with Tom, who really fancied himself as a Roman gladiator; with Charlie, bare-chested and sporting a *Gloves Off* sticker in a rather delicate position; and with half a dozen guys whose names she didn't even know, but who clearly saw themselves as inter-galactic travellers. She'd taken some stunning pictures for Izzy's birthday album, done a couple of caricatures of the guys Sophie and Bianca were drooling over, and drunk rather more than perhaps she should have done. But one thing was missing.

There was no sign of Ludo or Summer.

'I told you she wouldn't come,' Izzy reminded her smugly. 'But would you listen?' She smirked. 'Just because you're swanning off to Casa whatever with her, don't think you understand her. No one does.'

In desperation, Caitlin grabbed her mobile phone and began texting.

Where r u?

She paused and added, *U r missing gr8 party.*

She zapped the message on its way and turned round to find Tom holding a bottle of vodka in one hand, the other stretched out to grab hold of her.

'Come on,' he said, dragging her towards the stairs that led up from the basement to the main entrance hall. 'Conga time – it's another Izzy tradition.'

'On account of her being a total show-off,' Bianca cut in. 'She wants the whole Crescent to see that it's her birthday!'

'Last year,' Sophie added, 'she stopped the traffic for five whole minutes!'

'Round everyone up!' Izzy ordered. 'No dropouts!'

Caitlin had just reached the hallway when her mobile bleeped.

C u in 5. Sum

Her heart soared. They were coming! Now was the moment – did she dare do it? Would it be over the top? No, of course it wouldn't – she had read enough society magazines to know that the more off the wall you were the better you fitted in.

Do this and she'd be noticed by everyone who mattered.

She darted for the stairs that led to Izzy's bedroom.

'Hey, Caitlin, the conga!' Tom called.

'Two minutes!' she yelled back and scooted to the bathroom.

'Caitlin! Oh my God, what's happened?'

Bianca stared at her, open mouthed.

'You're wet!' Sophie gasped. 'And what's that in your hair?'

'I get it! Oh, that's so cool!' Izzy exclaimed admiringly, her arms hooked firmly round Jamie's waist. 'Get it everyone? She's Rose, right – the Kate Winslet character in *Titanic*? And the ship's gone down and she's drowning.'

She giggled as everyone turned. Caitlin's white dress was soaking wet, clinging to her curvaceous figure and showing clearly the outline of the skimpy white bikini underneath. Caitlin had threaded thin strands of seaweed from the beach through her wet hair, spread a little glue to the shoulders of the dress and sprinkled sand on it, and, as a final touch, dropped a couple of pink shells into her cleavage. Her *pièce de résistance* was the lifebelt (actually an old rubber ring from swimming-lesson days) with the words *Who will save me?* scribbled on in scarlet lipstick.

She was conscious of a load of admiring glances, not least from the guys, some of whom were edging closer to her. It was Tom whose arms went round her waist and whose lips began exploring the back of her neck.

'I'll be your saviour,' he murmured, nibbling her earlobe. 'And I think you need serious mouth-to-mouth resuscitation. Over a long period of time!'

Suddenly, the chatter and laughter was broken by a loud shrilling. Someone had their finger on the doorbell and they were not about to remove it.

'Let's hope whoever it is has brought more booze,' Izzy shouted.

'It'll be Ludo and Summer,' Caitlin said, trying to wriggle out of Tom's sweaty grasp. Perfect timing. The dress was clinging in all the right places; Ludo couldn't fail to be impressed.

'Come on, you lot!' shouted Izzy, grabbing hold of Jamie. 'First to the door gets the fittest guy! De der-der-der-de derder . . .'

She conga-ed her way to the door, squeezing past Bianca who was glued lip to lip with Louis, snogging as if her life depended on it. Caitlin, relieved to be free of Tom, grabbed the nearest bottle to top up her glass.

And that was when Izzy flung open the door.

For one awful moment, Caitlin thought a bomb had gone off. The blinding flash made her blink and reel backwards, straight into Tom's arms.

'Bloody hell!' she heard him exclaim. 'What the—?'

His expletives were drowned in a babble of voices from the front step. As Caitlin's vision cleared, she realised that a cluster of press photographers and reporters were crowding towards the door, cameras flashing and microphones being thrust forward.

This is it, she thought excitedly. It could be *Tatler*, *Hello!*, even *Harpers*, maybe . . .

Izzy seemed frozen to the spot, so Caitlin pushed forward, hoping that she would be in close up on the front cover of a glossy.

'We'd like a comment from your father – is he here?' one of the reporters asked, calling over Caitlin's shoulder to where Izzy was standing.

'Or would it be fair to say he's hiding his head in shame?' shouted another. 'Thought he could keep his memos under wraps, did he? Threatening school cutbacks on the nation, pontificating about bad parenting – and all the time he and his family splurge out on a—'

Caitlin was beginning to realise that this was not your usual society interview.

'My father's out,' Izzy shouted angrily. 'This is a private party and I'd be grateful if you'd respect our privacy.'

Caitlin had never heard her friend talk like this before. It was almost as if she'd pressed a play button and a recorded message was popping out of her mouth.

'Looks like you're having a pretty lively time here,' a thin guy with a microphone remarked. 'Parents out, teens raving . . . You're Isabella, I take it?'

Another flash dazzled Caitlin's eyes at the very moment Tom decided to grab her and hold her to him in a somewhat drunken embrace.

'So where are they this time?' demanded another one. 'Using tax-payers' money to buy themselves another night on the tiles?'

'They're at a ball at the Pavilion.' Izzy suddenly sounded small and scared.

'The Pavilion!' the guy yelled, and as one the posse turned and began clattering down the steps. 'Let's split, guys! Get over to the Pavilion, pronto!'

The paparazzi were already turning their backs on the house, shouting to one another and running down the steps on to the pavement.

'Hang on!' Izzy was about to slam the door shut when Summer, dressed in tennis whites and with a racquet in one hand, ran up the steps two at a time.

'About time,' Caitlin teased, looking over Summer's shoulder in an attempt to spot Ludo. 'What kept you?'

'You don't want to know,' Summer said quietly. 'Happy birthday, Izzy!'

She tapped Izzy on the shoulder and thrust a parcel into her hands. 'Did I miss the birthday photos? I thought I wasn't going to get past that lot – you certainly got maximum coverage this year. What a crowd!'

'I suppose you think that's funny,' muttered Izzy. 'Look, thanks for the present – but I've got to make a phone call.'

Summer glanced at Caitlin and raised an eyebrow.

'What's up with her?' she asked. 'And why are you soaking wet?'

'Why are you wearing tennis gear?' Caitlin returned. 'And where's Ludo?'

'Oh this – I'm, well, from that film, you know – *Wimbledon?*' she said hastily. 'And Ludo's gone to a movie with a mate – why?'

'But Izzy said she'd invited him . . .'

'She did, but no way would my brother do the fancy-dress bit, not for anyone.'

Caitlin's heart sank. Her own brother was prepared to dress up if it meant being with Izzy. Ludo clearly hadn't given her a second thought. All her efforts had been for nothing. He had been imprinted on her heart forever and what was she to him? A fleeting memory. If that.

'Caitlin, you're shivering,' Summer said, chucking her tennis racquet to one side.

'What's with the drowning rat bit?'

'Nothing,' mumbled Caitlin. 'Just something that seemed like a good idea at the time.'

'So what took you so long?' Caitlin asked as they headed down to the basement disco. 'The party started ages ago.'

'I know.' Summer shrugged. 'To be honest, I wasn't going to come – I hate hanging out at things like this without . . .'

She stopped mid-sentence and bit her lip.

'Without Ludo?' Caitlin asked.

'*Ludo*? Why would I want to hang out with my brother?' Summer asked.

'Well, who then?' Caitlin looked at her, noticing the flush creeping up her neck and behind her ears. 'You're hiding something. I can tell.'

Summer lowered her voice.

'Listen, if I tell you the whole story, you have to promise on your life that you won't say a word to a living soul.'

'I promise,' Caitlin said, sensing that she was about to be let in on one big secret.

'Well, about six months ago—'

'Hey, stop all this girly talk!' Tom lurched up to Caitlin, grabbed her and planted a rather beery kiss on her lips. 'Come and dance, sexy!'

'Tom, stop it!' Caitlin pulled away. 'I'm talking to Summer.'

'It's OK, you go ahead.' Summer shrugged. 'It's nothing, anyway.'

'See?' Tom laughed. 'What could possibly be more important than you and me partying big time?'

Caitlin was about to tell him where to go, but one glance at Summer assured her that she'd missed the moment. She'd just have to make sure that they had time alone again pretty soon.

Because she was certain that something really mysterious was going on. And if there was one thing she loved, it was a good mystery.

'Great party,' Caitlin said to Izzy at midnight as she hunted for her bag in Izzy's bedroom. 'I'm bushed – my feet feel like I've trekked across continents!'

She eyed Izzy questioningly.

'You OK?'

'Why did I do that? Why did I mess up?' Izzy replied, and Caitlin noticed that she was close to tears.

'What are you on about? It's been a brill party! Oh – you haven't had a row with Jamie, have you?'

'Of course not. I mean, telling the press where my parents were,' Izzy said. 'Apparently they gate-crashed the ball at the Pavilion and took loads of photos while Dad was . . . well, you know . . . having a good time. So I get Mum screaming at me down the phone for making it all more public than it needed to be, saying I've let the side down . . .'

'That's not fair,' Caitlin objected. 'What else could you have done?'

'Kept my mouth shut, according to my mother,' Izzy replied. 'You just don't know how lucky you are, Caitlin. You can go home to a normal family and do what the hell you like and no one will give a toss.'

She slumped down on the end of the bed.

'It's very hard being famous,' she sighed as the front door slammed downstairs and the sound of chattering drifted up from the pavement below. 'Such pressure.'

'Don't worry, it's not like the press are going to be interested in *you*, is it?' Caitlin reasoned. 'It's your dad they're interested in. What do they want to talk to him about?'

'Oh, the usual – me going to a posh school while his department cut back money to schools, and when they're tired of that one it's all about the fact that my parents like to live life, enjoy themselves, drive fast cars . . .'

She flicked a strand of hair behind her ear. 'Sometimes, I wish I was you.'

'Me?' Caitlin laughed. 'Hey, that wouldn't work – you couldn't snog Jamie if you were me!'

Instead of the laugh that Caitlin had hoped to produce, Izzy's face fell and every last trace of bravado faded.

'You don't think Jamie will go off me – you know, when the press start on about stuff . . .'

The pleading note in Izzy's voice wasn't lost on Caitlin.

'He's not that shallow – he's dead keen on you. He's never been like this with any other girl.'

'Really? You mean it? You're not just saying that to make me feel better?'

Caitlin shook her head.

'By the way,' she asked casually, 'what are you up to this holiday?'

'Sod all, probably,' Izzy muttered.

'If I let you into a secret,' Caitlin said hastily, 'will you promise faithfully not to tell Jamie I said anything?'

'Go on then – what?' Suddenly Izzy was all eagerness.

'He wants the two of you to go on holiday together,' Caitlin announced.

'Oh my God – it's not true? Really? When? Where?' Izzy gasped. 'We could go to Mauritius – it's so cool, you get little thatched houses on stilts – or maybe Bali! I've always wanted—'

'Hang on,' Caitlin interrupted. 'Jamie's not Bill Gates, you know. But he's got this plan – and you've got to look surprised when he tells you, OK? Because it's not quite all sorted yet. And it's going to be great, but trust me, long haul is out!'

'OK.' Izzy nodded eagerly. 'So when's he going to tell me?'

'Soon,' Caitlin assured her. 'I'm sure it'll be soon.'

'Do it now, OK?' Jamie whispered to Caitlin, glancing over his shoulder to where Summer and a cluster of others were waiting for cabs outside Izzy's house. 'Ask her about the holiday.'

He glanced at his watch. 'I'm relying on you. I'm going to see that Izzy's OK – don't let me down!'

'Your brother seems really nice,' Summer remarked, scanning the oncoming traffic for a taxi.

'He is, in small doses.' Caitlin smiled. 'Actually, he's much easier to live with now he's so in *lurve!*'

'I hope he doesn't get hurt,' Summer commented. 'I

mean, Izzy's OK, but she's just out for a bit of fun and a good laugh.'

'She hasn't got much to laugh about right now, though,' Caitlin remarked. 'Jamie was saying that he really thinks she's going to need to get away from her parents for a bit, with all that's going on with the press and stuff.'

She waited, hoping that Summer would cotton on.

'So, is anyone else coming to Casa Vernazza?' she went on when Summer didn't respond.

'Not if I can help it,' Summer said. 'Dad keeps on about getting a gang together, because he wants me to have fun, but I reckon it's just an excuse to get a load of people around so that Gabriella can show off to them.'

She pulled a face. 'See, there's a whole heap of stuff I've got to sort out this holiday – that's partly why I need you there. You're kind of, well, sensitive, and not in your face.'

Caitlin glowed. 'Is this about what you were going to tell me?' she began.

Summer nodded.

'Partly,' she said. 'But not now and not here – I'll tell you when we get to Italy. You'll understand better once we're there.'

She sighed. 'Trouble is, if I don't invite some mates, Dad'll probably take matters into his own hands and drag the cousins over, and that, believe me, would be the pits. Anyone would be better than them.'

'In that case,' said Caitlin with a smile, 'I think this is one problem I can help you with.'

Sorted!' Caitlin told Jamie half an hour later, as they drove home. 'You owe me – she wasn't exactly keen. Izzy isn't her favourite person in the universe.'

'I can't see why,' Jamie protested. 'She's great – she's fun, she's witty, she's got this really soft side . . . '

'OK, OK – you run the fan club, I'll tell you the rules,' said Caitlin, laughing. 'You two do your own thing, right? Summer and I have got stuff to sort out.'

'What stuff?'

'Art project,' Caitlin told him hastily. 'We'll be working flat out. On our own. OK? We don't want Izzy cribbing all our ideas.'

'Suits me.' Jamie grinned. 'Couldn't be better. As kid sisters go, I reckon you're OK.'

🎕 CHAPTER 4 🎕

'Circumstances change, opinions alter.'
(Jane Austen, *Northanger Abbey*)

'I CAN'T BELIEVE IT, CAITLIN – HOW COULD YOU? HOW could you make such an exhibition of yourself?'

Mrs Morland sat at the kitchen table, staring in disbelief at the photograph in the centre page of the newspaper. While the foreground was taken up by a very angry-looking Izzy, it was the image of Caitlin, glass in hand, lolling in Tom's arms with a wet dress clinging to every curve, that her mother kept stabbing with her finger.

'Toeing the party line! Like father, like daughter; teens in wild party while minister preaches about standards . . .'

Her mother looked close to tears.

'Mum, it wasn't how it looks,' Caitlin insisted. 'We were just—'

'Look at you!' her father butted in, leaning over his wife's shoulder. 'I can see your underwear! And what have you done to your hair?'

'Hey, let's look!' Jamie shuffled into the kitchen in his

bathrobe, hair tousled and stubble on his chin. 'Wow! That's some picture.'

'This is not something to proud of!' his mother retorted. 'And as for you, James, what were you doing, letting your sister prance around, swigging alcohol . . .'

'Oh come on, Mum, I'm not her nanny,' Jamie reasoned. 'Anyway, it was no big deal. We were just having a laugh, then the press barged in looking for Izzy's dad and . . .'

'Ah yes,' sighed his dad. 'Isabella's father. The papers are having a field day over him.'

He tossed a couple of tabloids on to the table.

'So I should think!' Mrs Morland blurted out. 'He stands up in the Commons preaching about how we should all take responsibility for our children and then he lets his daughter host a drunken party and—'

'Now wait, Lynne,' Caitlin's father said hastily. 'If I've learned one thing in all my years in law, it's not to believe everything you read in the press. As I keep telling Caitlin when she wastes her money on those awful gossip magazines, if it's in the press, the chances are it's at least fifty per cent incorrect.'

'Precisely!' Caitlin shouted in triumph and grabbed her opportunity. 'Just like that photograph – it looks so much worse than it was. I wasn't drunk – I was so startled I fell back into Tom's arms when the flash bulbs went off.'

'So why were you soaking wet, answer me that one?' her mother demanded.

'I – er . . .'

'Come on, Mum,' Jamie broke in quickly, 'you can hardly blame Caitlin for the fact that some idiot got silly and hurled a jug of water over her, can you? These things happen at parties.'

He winked at her as their parents glanced at one another.

'I suppose you have a point,' Mr Morland said reluctantly. 'On this occasion, we will say no more about it – but just let it be a lesson to you. You never know who's watching you.'

'Can I go now?' Caitlin asked. 'Summer and me—'

'Summer and *I*,' corrected her father.

'Whatever. We've arranged to meet up and do some shopping – bikinis and stuff for the holiday.'

'Oh no,' her mother replied firmly. 'In view of all this . . .' She pointed to the newspaper and shuddered. '. . . you are not going anywhere with that crowd.'

Caitlin stared at her, aghast.

'Mum, you can't do that! You promised. You can't go back on your word now.'

'You're very naïve – that much has been made *quite* clear – and going off on your own with perfect strangers is now just not on. At your age, a family holiday is much better – I've said it all along.'

'She won't be on her own. Because I'm going too,' Jamie announced.

'You? You never said.'

'I couldn't get a word in edgeways!' he pointed out. 'Summer invited me last night, at the party. And Izzy's going to come, too.'

Bad move, thought Caitlin. Not a good idea.

'You? And Isabella?' Mrs Morland looked horror-struck. 'But Jamie, you hardly know the girl.'

'Mum, this is the twenty-first century.' Jamie sighed. 'You don't have to know someone for months before you get – well, before you hold hands.'

'But her family – I mean, you can see for yourself.' His mother stabbed at the newspaper again. 'What sort of example are they?'

'What her parents do is not Izzy's fault,' Jamie retorted.

'True, but your mother does have a point, Jamie,' his father remarked. 'I'm not at all sure that you're wise to get too involved with all these upper-class, trust-fund types. I said when Caitlin started at that school, that they're not our sort, they don't have our moral parameters and—'

Mr Morland stopped in mid-sentence as the doorbell rang.

'I expect,' Caitlin's mother put in, looking reprovingly at Caitlin, 'that will be someone from the village, waving a newspaper and gloating over your behaviour. Edward, you get it.'

Her husband sighed and went to the door.

'You want what?' they heard Caitlin's father exclaim. 'Well, you can go on wanting. No comment – none whatsoever!'

The front door slammed with such force that the ornaments on the hall table rattled. Mr Morland stormed back into the room.

'Bloody cheek!'

'Dad!' Jamie and Caitlin exclaimed in unison. The one thing not allowed in their house was any form of swearing.

'Edward, what is it?' Caitlin's mother asked.

'Local paper wanting to talk to Caitlin,' he replied. 'Apparently, someone recognised her photo and now the *Chronicle* want one of those "I was there and this is what really happened" pieces.'

'I don't mind,' Caitlin burst out eagerly. 'I took loads of photos. Maybe they'd buy some – even do a double-page spread!'

One look at her father's face told her that saying any more would be a very bad idea.

Within seconds, the doorbell was ringing again.

'Oh, for pity's sake!' Mr Morland stormed out of the room. They heard the front door being yanked open.

'I thought I made it quite clear— oh. I'm sorry. I didn't realise . . . Yes, of course, come in, my dear.'

Caitlin and Jamie both started at the sound of a familiar voice; a moment later, their father returned, looking acutely embarrassed and closely followed by a very tearful Izzy.

'I'm so sorry, really I am.' Izzy sniffed, dabbing her eyes with a tissue and accepting the glass of lemonade that Caitlin's mother offered her. 'I should have phoned before I came, but it's just that, well, Caitlin's my closest friend and you're such lovely people – and I didn't know . . .'

She's good, I'll give her that, thought Caitlin, as she watched her mother soften before her very eyes.

'. . . and Jamie said if there was ever anything he could do for me and, right now, just being with him would help so much . . .'

She looked up at Caitlin's brother and gave him a watery smile. Jamie put a protective arm around her shoulder and glared defiantly at his parents.

'I thought, where can I go to get away from all the phone calls – they've even got my mobile number and . . . well, here was the only place really. So I called a cab and just came.'

She sniffed and pressed her lips together.

'I'm sorry if it's imposing – only Dad's holed up with the PM . . .'

She paused to see the effect that her name-dropping had on the assembled company.

'You mean . . . the *Prime Minister?*' Caitlin's mother satisfied her urge.

'Mmm,' Izzy went on, 'and Mum keeps crying . . .'

'Of course you're not imposing,' Mrs Morland insisted. 'I'm glad you felt able to come to us. Whatever is going on with your parents, it shouldn't be allowed to affect you. Isn't that right, Edward?'

'Absolutely.' He nodded.

Parents, thought Caitlin, are so two-faced at times.

'I'll just go and water those tomatoes,' muttered her father, getting to his feet with more alacrity than he had shown all morning. 'Leave you in peace.'

'Edward . . .' Mrs Morland protested, but he'd already disappeared through the back door.

'Of course, Dad's done nothing wrong, nothing at all,' Izzy continued firmly. 'He just likes to unwind from the stress of being in office. And he wasn't really flirting at the Ball, it was just . . .'

She stopped, clearly worried that she'd said too much.

'Never mind all that,' Jamie burst out. 'How do you feel about a holiday?'

'Fat chance now,' Izzy replied. 'Dad will say—'

'Not with them, with me,' Jamie went on. 'You and me are off to Italy.'

'Italy? You and me? What do you mean?' Izzy gave the impression of being a cerebrally-challenged four-year-old as her eyes widened and she clamped a hand to her mouth. 'I don't understand.'

Caitlin appreciated why Izzy had been awarded a drama scholarship.

'Summer's invited us. All we have to do is pay for our air fare.'

'Summer? We're going with Summer?' Izzy's face fell.

'That's OK, isn't it?' Jamie suddenly looked anxious. 'I mean, we'll do lots of stuff on our own. You can have all the privacy you want.'

Izzy recovered herself.

'It's like a dream come true,' she cried. 'Oh, I can't believe it – you've saved my life!'

She looked at Jamie with the sort of expression most people reserve for new-born babies or small spaniels with floppy ears.

'And your parents, dear?' Mrs Morland queried. 'They won't mind you going off with Jamie and Caitlin?'

'Course not,' Izzy assured her. 'They're really laid-back and open-minded – they let me do more or less what I like.'

'What a surprise,' Mrs Morland muttered.

Izzy jumped up and grabbed Jamie's arm.

'Come on – let's go into Brighton and celebrate! Ice creams on the pier and then I've got some serious holiday shopping to attend to!'

'Me too,' Caitlin added quickly. 'I'll just go and get my purse.'

'Can I take your car, Mum?' Jamie asked. 'If all three of us are going . . .'

'I suppose,' his mother said, tossing him the car keys.

'Do you have to tag along?' Izzy hissed at Caitlin, as Jamie went to fetch the car. 'I wanted Jamie to myself and—'

'Hey, hang on!' Caitlin argued. 'I'll have you know that you wouldn't be going if it wasn't for me – Jamie got me to set it up with Summer. And don't let my parents know, but he's intending to take you off somewhere else most of the time. Summer's just the alibi.'

Izzy flung her arms round her friend's neck and hugged her.

'So you were right – he really does love me! Oh, I'm so happy!'

'Won't you . . . well, be worried about what's going on at home?' Caitlin asked. 'You know, with your dad and . . .'

'Oh for pity's sake, don't keep going on about it!' Izzy snapped. 'My father can wriggle out of anything, trust me. Of all the people in the universe you need to worry about, he's not one of them.'

'So come on, Izzy, tell me about Summer's mother!' Caitlin insisted, after Jamie had escaped to buy a car magazine and they were slumped outside Café Nero with cappucinos and chocolate brownies, waiting for Summer to arrive. 'You've been hinting at stuff for ages. What's with all the secrecy?'

'Well, I don't know all the details but my dad used to play golf with a guy who worked with Summer's dad, right? Apparently, she was out walking in the middle of a thunderstorm and she fell, hit her head and that was it.'

'How awful!'

'And,' Izzy went on, dipping her tongue into the froth on her coffee, 'she lay there for two days before anyone found the body. What do you make of that?'

'My God!' Caitlin gasped.

'Of course, Summer said it was a tragic accident, but she would, wouldn't she? I mean, would you want the world to know that your mother drank herself into an early grave?'

'You never said – you mean, she was an alcoholic?'

'I guess. I mean, I don't actually know for sure,' Izzy confessed, 'but this guy told Dad that she used to party like mad and get really off her face.'

'Poor Summer,' sighed Caitlin. 'That must be why she hates parties – you know, bad memories and all that.'

'I never thought of that,' Izzy remarked pensively. 'You're quite clued up sometimes, aren't you?'

Caitlin suddenly remembered that Summer had asked for a white wine at Mango Monkey's and mentioned all the drinks she enjoyed in Italy. Could that mean, just possibly, that poor Summer had inherited her mother's genetic profile? Maybe she was heading the same way. Maybe that's why she was a loner – all the magazines said that people with issues often hid themselves away for ages at a time to try to disguise their problems . . .

'I'll have a chat with her when we're on holiday,' Caitlin said. 'Find out . . .'

'Not if you value your life, you won't!' Izzy exclaimed. 'I told you – it's a total no-go area with her. You're much better to keep quiet about it.'

'She'll tell me things,' Caitlin assured her. 'We're on the same wavelength.'

'Really?' Izzy's tone changed. 'That's not something I'd be bragging about.'

Caitlin was unloading her shopping on to her bed when her mobile rang. *Private call.*

She frowned, flipping open the lid. All her mates were programmed in with their names.

'Hello?'

'Pretty cool picture in the paper, wasn't it?' Her heart sank. It was Tom.

'Not from where I'm standing,' she replied. 'My parents went ballistic.'

'Well, I think you looked really sexy,' he said, laughing. 'I've cut you out and stuck you on the wall above my bed.' He cleared his throat. 'Look, I was thinking. How do you fancy a trip to Southampton next weekend? That mate I told you about – he's sailing his boat down there this week and having a party on Saturday night.'

'Sorry, I'll be in Italy,' she said, enjoying the way it

tripped off her tongue.

'*Italy*? How come?' Tom sounded as if it was incomprehensible that she would go anywhere without first consulting him.

Caitlin gave him a few sparse details.

'And that Ludo guy? I suppose he'll be there.'

'Sure he will,' replied Caitlin.

'So what about me and you?'

'There *is* no me and you,' Caitlin pointed out. 'Not yet, anyway.'

'So you mean – there could be? When you get back?'

'Well, I . . .'

'I do like you, you know.' With each day that passed, it seemed he was less up himself.

'I like you too,' Caitlin replied, because she was going away soon and because she didn't want to hurt his feelings. 'I'll see you when I get back.'

And hopefully by then, she thought, the entire universe will know that Ludo and me are an item and no one else stands a chance.

'Bye Tom, take care.'

She could afford to be magnanimous with a fortnight in the company of Ludo Tilney stretching ahead of her.

Caitlin's mother calmed down a bit after Sir Magnus telephoned her from Heathrow Airport.

'Such a charming man,' she enthused. 'He was so sorry not to be able to meet us, but they're flying out today to prepare the house for all you young people. I told him you could be a bit headstrong . . .'

'Mum, you didn't!' Caitlin gasped.

'. . . and he said that he would keep an eye on you all and ring if there was anything at all to worry about. So that's nice, isn't it?'

'Compared to what?' Caitlin asked. 'A playgroup outing? Mum, you are so embarrassing, it's unreal.'

'I just care, that's all,' her mother said.

'I know.' Caitlin smiled, hugging her. 'But just care *quietly* for the next couple of weeks, yeah?'

CHAPTER 5

'A good-looking girl with an affectionate heart cannot fail of attracting a clever young man.'
(Jane Austen, *Northanger Abbey*)

'YOU'RE NOT SCARED, ARE YOU?' LUDO TOUCHED CAITLIN'S hand as she gripped the armrest of her aircraft seat.

'It's the going up and coming down bits I hate – once we're up there, I'll be fine,' she murmured.

She flinched and closed her eyes as the jet engines revved and the aircraft gathered speed down the runway. So much for looking cool and sophisticated; she could feel the sweat breaking out on her forehead and all she could do was hold her breath and pray that the aeroplane would actually get off the ground before it careered into the perimeter fence.

'Lift off!' Ludo said, nudging her elbow. She opened one eye and saw him grinning at her in amusement. 'If this holds such terrors for you, how on earth will you cope with Luigi and his Lamborghini? Or me and Gina?'

'Who?'

It had never occurred to her that Ludo might have a girlfriend waiting in Italy. Her stomach, already behaving in a very unpredictable manner as the aircraft banked and headed southwards, lurched even more at the thought of losing him before she'd even got him.

'Well, Luigi's been with our family for as long as I can remember – he must be seventy if he's a day. He'll be meeting us at the airport. Drives like a maniac – just wait till you're speeding along round hairpin bends with him. This plane will seem as safe as a rocking horse.'

'And Gina?' Caitlin swallowed hard and tried to look as if she couldn't give a hoot about this woman.

'Now, Gina you have to see,' he told her seriously. 'She is exquisite. And such fun to take out. Last month I took her down to Portofino and I swear to you, even there, everyone was staring at her, she's so gorgeous.'

He smiled and touched Caitlin's hand.

'Tell you what,' he said, 'we'll go and take her out first thing tomorrow, OK? You'll love her.'

I doubt it very much, thought Caitlin miserably.

'So,' he asked later, as the steward stopped with a trolley of drinks, 'are you feeling better now? What will you have to drink?'

'Orange juice, please,' she mumbled, grabbing the latest copy of *Prego* from the pile of celebrity magazines she'd bought at the airport and pretending to be absorbed in the fate of the stars of the latest TV reality show. She couldn't believe it: all her dreams of romance under a Mediterranean sun, of kisses stolen under the light of the moon, of declarations of future intent pledged with a kiss in an orange grove – all gone. He'd got a girlfriend and she was gorgeous. If only she'd known . . .

'Oh my goodness!' Ludo stabbed a finger at the magazine, his mouth dropping open. 'Look at that – *Pop star in love triangle with ex-nun and supermodel!*'

'I know,' Caitlin said. 'It's unbelievable – he actually got engaged to Tanya Christy while he was living with this woman who got thrown out of a convent. What do you think of that?'

'Oh my God! That is so amazing! It can't be true,' Ludo gasped.

'No, honestly, it must be, because it was in the *Sun* too, only I didn't get it because there was this big bit on the front page about Izzy's dad and I thought it might upset her.'

She flicked the page. 'And look, they're doing this whole series. Next week it's about that girl who was in *Cry Wolf* – did you know she had a sex change eight years ago? They're going to do a total exposé of the whole thing . . .'

'How am I going to last until you get the next issue?' Ludo laughed, wiping his forehead dramatically. 'Oh, the suspense, the angst . . .'

Caitlin felt a total fool. He had been sending her up the whole time and she'd fallen for it.

'I suppose you think I'm an idiot, enjoying stuff like this,' she mumbled. 'It's mainly because of the photographs – you know, from an artistic point of view.'

She could see he didn't believe a word of it, which was hardly surprising.

'I do read serious stuff too.'

'Of course you do,' Ludo teased. 'What could be more serious than footballers' wives with breast implants!'

He picked up his book and began reading, an amused grin spreading across his face. Caitlin noticed that the book was one of those complicated political espionage thrillers that always had her lost by the third chapter.

For the next ten minutes Caitlin stared out of the window. No way was he going to be interested in her, other than as a rather silly friend of his sister. She'd been to Summer's house twice in the last few days, gossiping about holiday plans and stuff, and he'd hardly glanced in her direction. Now, she knew why; this Gina was probably some stunning Italian girl who read intellectual novels and never, ever watched TV because she was too busy discussing politics. Caitlin knew she'd messed up before they'd even landed; so much for her dreams of romance. She wanted to cry, but unlike Izzy, she couldn't do that halfway attractively so she just stared at the clouds and wished that she could wind the clock back.

Ten minutes later, when Ludo had got up to wander down the aisle and talk to Jamie and Izzy, she decided to challenge Summer.

'Why didn't you tell me?' Caitlin hissed, leaning across the aisle. 'About Gina?'

Summer looked up from her book and frowned.

'I didn't give it a thought – why would you be interested?'

'Oh, come off it – you must have guessed I . . . well, I quite like Ludo and . . .'

Summer burst out laughing.

'I thought you did! And you're bothered about Gina? Because you think Ludo's in love with her?'

'He didn't stop going on about her – he says she's gorgeous,' Caitlin insisted.

'Well, she is,' Summer agreed. 'And I suppose you could say Ludo's besotted with her.'

'Great,' Caitlin muttered. 'He even had the nerve to suggest we all went out together.'

Summer laughed again.

'So? I think that's rather sweet.'

'I'm so glad *you* find it funny.'

Summer shook her head. 'Oh, Caitlin, don't look so miserable – *Gina's* a boat!'

'A boat?' Caitlin stared at her in disbelief.

'A speedboat,' Summer confirmed. 'Dead classy, if you're into that sort of thing. Ludo's godfather died last year and left his boat to Ludo. Freddie was dead cheesed off, I can tell you.'

She picked up her book again.

'You're into boats, aren't you?' she remarked. 'You said how you go sailing with your family.'

'Mmm,' murmured Caitlin. 'Love them.'

She thought perhaps at this point it was best to gloss over the fact that she had embellished, just a little, the story of the family's preoccupation with sailing. She wasn't sure that the annual half-day round the Isle of Wight on *The Wight Princess* was in quite the same league.

'That's good.' Summer winked at her. 'Because with Ludo, it's a case of love me, love my boat!'

* * *

'Oh no! Why did *she* have to come?'

Summer stopped dead, shielding her eyes from the bright Italian sun glinting on the windows of the arrival hall at Genoa Airport.

She gestured to a tall, slender woman in white Capri pants and a gold silk baby-doll top, waving to them enthusiastically from behind the crush barrier.

'I guess she had to, didn't she?' Ludo reasoned. 'We can't all fit in one car with Luigi.'

'Well, no way am I driving all the way home with her and that's final,' Summer declared.

'I guess that's the new woman,' Caitlin whispered to Izzy, eyeing the chestnut hair and designer suntan. 'She's dead glamorous.'

'She may look good,' muttered Summer, overhearing them, 'but don't let that fool you. Underneath, she's a right conniving, manipulative cow.'

'Summer, don't start!' Ludo hissed at her as they got within earshot of Gabriella. 'This is a holiday, for heaven's sake – loosen up, can't you? Please? For the sake of the rest of us?'

Summer sighed.

'OK,' she agreed. 'I'm sorry – I'll do my best.'

'Darlings! You're here – isn't this lovely?' Gabriella threw her arms open expansively and beamed at them all. 'Now come along, introductions can wait. The cars are outside and I've got drinks on ice in the cool bags!'

Outside, Luigi, a small, gnome-like man with greying hair and skin like a wrinkled satsuma was waiting beside a bright yellow Lamborghini, a car that in an instant had Jamie away from Izzy's side and positively drooling over the hubcaps. Ludo began piling the luggage into the boot.

'Caitlin, what have you got in here?' he demanded as he attempted to lift her suitcase.

'It's my paints and extra camera lenses and stuff,' she explained apologetically.

'Paints?' Ludo repeated.

'You paint?' Gabriella exclaimed at the same moment. 'Summer didn't say.'

'Why should I?' Summer demanded. 'I don't have to provide a CV of all my friends.'

'No need to be prickly, darling,' Gabriella replied calmly. 'I just – well, you know what your father's like about the smell of oil paint and . . .'

'I do watercolours,' Caitlin said hastily, wondering why Summer's dad should have a problem with oil paint. 'And pastels sometimes. I'll be going out and about to paint – I won't be any trouble, I promise.'

'I'm sure you won't, sweetie,' Gabriella replied. 'Just best if you paint away from the villa, OK? Now then, let's get going. Mags is barbecuing this evening and I'm on salad duty!'

Ludo shoved Summer into the back of the Lamborghini with Izzy and Jamie and gestured to Caitlin to join him in Gabriella's sleek little open-top Alfa Romeo.

'We'll break you in gently,' he said, grinning. 'I don't think you'll cope with one of Luigi's high-speed car chases right now!'

Gabriella climbed into the driving seat.

'I've got to make a little detour, so I'll see you back at the house,' Gabriella called to Luigi. '*Arrivederci!*'

With every mile, Caitlin's happiness doubled. She couldn't believe that she was sitting, thigh touching thigh, with the fittest guy in the universe, sipping a chilled Prosecco and feeling the warm Mediterranean sun on her cheeks. Not even the knowledge that those same cheeks would, in all probability, be covered in a mass of freckles by the time they reached their destination, could dampen her excitement.

'Have you been to Italy before, Caitlin?' Gabriella asked as they left the busy streets of Genoa behind them and gathered speed along the spectacular coast road, rugged mountains rising steeply behind them and the sun sparkling on the sort of sea Caitlin had only seen on postcards.

'Never,' Caitlin admitted. 'I just can't wait to explore it all.'

'Well, I've got loads of plans,' Gabriella assured her. 'There are some wonderful shops, and we'll go to Portofino for lunch at the Splendido, and then I thought we could take the boat trip to all the villages of the Cinque Terre and of course, if you're into art, I must take you to the Palazzo Reale in Genoa—'

'Gaby, you don't have to take care of us,' Ludo cut in firmly. 'We've got plenty of plans of our own.'

'Sure you have,' Gaby acknowledged, turning off the coast road up a steep and winding lane, and pulling up outside a large, pink painted villa. 'It's just that your father thought . . . Oh well, I'm sure you're right. Look, I've just got to drop off a present for a friend of mine – won't be long!'

'Great,' Ludo said, the moment Gabriella had shut the car door. 'I've been wanting a moment with you alone ever since we boarded the plane.'

Caitlin's heart flipped as he leaned closer to her.

'Look, this is a bit tricky and I don't quite know how to put it . . .'

He's going to tell me he fancies me, Caitlin thought, trying to keep a cool expression on her face.

'Go ahead,' she invited.

'I'm really glad you've come,' he said, and Caitlin's heart swelled. This was it. This was going to be the declaration of love. 'It's just what Summer needs.'

'*Summer?*'

Ludo nodded.

'She spends far too much time brooding over stuff,' he went on, keeping one eye on the doorway of the villa where Gabriella was talking to an elderly woman in a floral print dress. 'Like this whole thing with Gaby, for instance.'

'I know she said she didn't like her, but she seems nice enough to me,' Caitlin said, hiding her disappointment at his choice of topic.

'Exactly!' Ludo looked at her approvingly. 'Dad's happy for the first time in ages – well, ever since Mum died really.'

He swallowed hard and took a deep breath.

'Mum dying was awful for all of us,' he said. 'But

{ 89 }

Summer – well, she's never really been the same since. She – well, she almost had a kind of collapse. She missed loads of school, did atrociously in her SATS, cut herself off from her friends. That's why she changed schools; music's her thing and Mulberry Court was a new start – well, you know all about that. But it seems the older she gets, the worse it appears to affect her.'

As he spoke, he suddenly looked a lot younger. He kept clenching and unclenching his hands and chewing on his bottom lip like a nervous schoolboy. Caitlin wanted to enfold him in her arms, but she thought it was perhaps a little too soon for that.

Gabriella was still talking to the old lady. Caitlin took a deep breath and seized her chance.

'So what actually happened?' Caitlin asked. 'To your mum, I mean.'

'She had a fall, fractured her skull and it killed her,' he replied abruptly. 'Anyway, it's over and well – it's something we don't talk about, OK?'

Ludo's expression was grim and he turned away, staring at a couple of goats tethered on the burnt lawn of the villa. 'It was over two years ago and life goes on, right?'

Caitlin hesitated. Of course, she had read all about the effects of unexpressed grief, and that could account for his abruptness, but perhaps, just possibly, Izzy was right. There was dark secret lurking in the history of the Tilney family.

She would have liked to have pressed him, insisting that these things had to be aired and telling him about that guy on Channel Four's *Passion Plantation* who ran amok during the live filming because the sight of a palm tree triggered a buried emotion about the death of his mother by a falling coconut. Sadly, before she could say a word, she heard Gabriella call out a shrill '*Arrivederci*, Sofia!' and head back towards the car.

'All I'm asking,' Ludo muttered hurriedly, his expression softening, 'is that – well, you try to get Summer to hang loose this holiday. Do girl stuff or whatever. Have a laugh. She's so uptight half the time and it's bad for her. Not much fun for the rest of us either.'

He dropped his voice as Gabriella reached the gate.

'I just want our lives to be normal again,' he muttered. 'Summer needs to accept that Gaby's a permanent fixture, whether she likes it or not. Get her to see it's the future that matters now. She might listen to you – after all, you are her best friend. Well, the only person she really talks about anyway.'

'OK, I'll do my best.' Caitlin nodded, delighted at her new-found status as the person the whole Tilney family could depend on to make the future easier. 'Leave it to me.'

'Oh wow!' For all her good intentions about remaining cool and sophisticated, Caitlin couldn't help exclaiming with delight as the car rounded the gravel drive and pulled up outside Casa Vernazza. The sprawling, red-roofed villa was surrounded on three sides by a wide veranda; swathes of bright pink-flowering bougainvillea grew up the white walls and a couple of marble Muses flanked the stone steps that led up to the front door.

'It's amazing – it's like something out of a movie,' Caitlin exclaimed.

'Definitely a *budget* movie,' Gabriella said with a laugh, pulling on the handbrake and flinging open the door. 'It's pretty, but it's falling down. Don't sneeze while you're here – some plaster might fall on your head!'

She turned to Summer and Izzy, who were coming down the front steps to greet them.

'I'll show the girls to their rooms, shall I?' she began.

'They're my friends – I'll do it,' Summer replied, and then, catching Ludo's eye, added, 'but thanks for offering.'

'Fine,' Gabriella replied with a shrug. 'And then why don't you all go and explore until suppertime? Drinks on the veranda at seven on the dot, supper al fresco at eight.'

She tossed her car keys at Luigi, who was unloading luggage from the boot of the Alfa Romeo.

'Put the car away, there's a dear,' she trilled. 'I simply have to go and take a shower – this heat is killing me.'

'I wish,' muttered Summer, sidling up to Caitlin. 'Come on, I'll show you and Izzy your rooms. Ludo can sort Jamie out.'

She set off up the wide stone steps leading to the front door, which stood open revealing a tiled hallway.

'Must you?' sighed Caitlin, as Izzy wrapped herself round Jamie and began kissing him urgently. 'For heaven's sake, you're going to find your bedroom, not leaving on a polar expedition!'

Reluctantly, Izzy pulled away from Jamie and blew him a kiss. Ludo winked at Caitlin and pulled a face, mouthing 'Sad or what?' behind Izzy's back. Caitlin sighed inwardly, guessing that it was too much to hope that sometime soon he'd be doing the same thing with her.

'This is so cool,' Caitlin breathed as Summer showed them one room after another, all with huge double doors leading on to terraces with views across olive groves and rooftops to the distant sea. The rugs in the dining room were fading and frayed at the edges, the sofas in the two sitting rooms were sagging – but all this, Caitlin thought, made the place even more perfect. It had a sense of timelessness about it. Besides, she'd read that 'old money' never purchased new stuff; even the Queen saved bits of old soap.

'So where's Jamie sleeping?' Izzy demanded.

'I told Gaby to put him in the Garden House,' Summer told her. 'Next to Freddie. I thought he'd be around now but apparently he's gone over to La Spezia for some bike spares. He should be back soon.'

'Freddie's here?' Izzy's face lit up. 'Great – he is such a laugh.'

'You know him? Oh yes, you met at Open Day,' Summer remarked.

'With the super soakers and the champagne, remember?' Izzy laughed. 'He was so cool.'

'Insane, more like,' Summer said, grinning. She opened a door and stood back to let Izzy through. 'This is your room – the bathroom's next door. And that's the Garden House, just across the courtyard.'

Izzy caught her eye and smiled.

'Perfect,' she said. 'Couldn't be better. This is going to be such a cool holiday.'

'You're in here,' Summer announced, flinging open a door and ushering Caitlin into a low-ceilinged bedroom with a sloping floor, whitewashed walls, and creamy voile curtains billowing in the late afternoon breeze. Caitlin sized up the brass ceiling fan, marble shower room and faded Loyd Loom chairs with a sigh of joy. 'I know it's not as big as Izzy's room,' Summer went on, 'but it's the only one with a balcony and my mum used to say the light here was perfect for painting.'

'Your mother was an artist?' Caitlin asked in surprise. Now she understood Gabriella's earlier concerns about painting.

Summer nodded. 'She was seriously good,' she said. 'She was going to have this big exhibition, but Dad wouldn't let her. Said it was too pretentious – like, can you imagine that?'

She flung open the doors to the balcony.

'If you like, I'll show you some of her stuff later.'

'Yes, please.' Caitlin nodded enthusiastically, stepping out on to the tiny balcony and gazing out across the courtyard shaded by lemon trees heavy with fruit. 'This is beautiful. But Summer, the trouble is, Gabriella said that I shouldn't paint in the house.'

'Ignore her,' Summer said. 'It's *my* home, not hers. Mum used to paint wherever she wanted – *when*ever she wanted. That's what real artists do.'

'You don't talk much about your mum,' Caitlin ventured, a little nervously.

'That's because at home everyone goes all stiff and upset, and at school . . .' She shrugged. 'Well, it's not the kind of thing you chat about to just anybody.'

She paused, the corners of her mouth twitching into a faint smile.

'She was a laugh, though – really good fun and not a bit like my friends' mothers. I mean, she'd get these crazy ideas. Like once, she woke me up in the middle of the night and said we were going on an adventure. We went up the hill behind the house and she made a fire and she taught me gypsy dances and then we slept up there till morning. It rained and we got soaked!'

Caitlin blinked, trying to picture her own mother doing anything as way-out.

'And another day, she decided me and her would have a picnic but we could only eat things beginning with L. She got really cross with me because I packed some lettuce and she wanted only stuff that started with an L in *Italian*. She threw a total wobbly.'

'She sounds fantastic, Summer. Can I ask . . . er, did she die out here? In Italy?' Caitlin held her breath and prayed that she wasn't overstepping the mark.

'Yes,' Summer said abruptly, glancing at her watch. 'Oh sugar, is that the time? Listen, will you promise me that whatever I tell you about stuff while you're here you won't breathe a word to anyone? Not Izzy, not Jamie, no one. I mean, if you can't keep a secret, just say so now.'

'Of course I can,' Caitlin vowed. 'We're in this – whatever it is – together.'

'Good,' Summer said decisively. 'So right now we're going down to the village, OK? You can unpack later.'

'Sure.' Caitlin grabbed her sun hat and slung her camera round her neck. 'Is Ludo coming?'

The moment the words had escaped her lips and she'd seen the amused smile on Summer's lips, she could have kicked herself.

'. . . and Izzy and Jamie?' she finished hurriedly, in the hopes that it would sound as if she was merely concerned for everyone's well-being.

'This is just you and me,' Summer replied firmly. 'Anyway, by now, my father will have dragged Ludo off to discuss crop yields or vine weevil or something equally riveting, so you're out of luck there.'

Caitlin tried to look totally disinterested.

'I didn't mean . . . well, I know that it must be hard for you, what with Izzy having Jamie, and me being with Ludo . . . Well, not *with* Ludo exactly . . .'

'. . . but fancying him like crazy,' Summer finished with a laugh. 'And no, it's not hard at all. You'll soon see.'

She opened the door and stepped out on to the galleried landing. 'Come on – no doubt Jamie and Izzy can keep themselves amused. I gave her that room for a reason – with a bit of luck, she'll work out pretty quickly that she can nip across the courtyard to Jamie's room without anyone knowing . . . that should keep them occupied!'

Caitlin giggled. 'And to think people say you're prudish,' she mused and then checked herself. 'I don't mean . . .'

'I know what people say, and I couldn't give a damn,' Summer replied. 'Now, come on – we've only got an hour before Gabriella starts insisting on communal jollity all over the place.'

'When we get to the village, you go off and do what you like, OK?' Summer began, as they followed a narrow path through terraced vineyards and olive groves, the sound of cicadas a constant background to their conversation. 'I'll show you where to meet me later.'

'Why can't we stay together?'

'I'm meeting someone, that's why,' Summer admitted. 'I haven't said anything to him about you—'

'*Him?*'

Caitlin's mind raced off at a tangent. Could this be the guy she'd thought Ludo was trying to protect his sister from? Surely it couldn't be, because he was in England, if he existed? But what if he was a *real* stalker, someone who would fly anywhere in the world to be near the object of his twisted affections? What if, in fact, Summer was the naïve and trusting victim, lured by his good looks, unsuspecting of his real motives . . .

'Who *is* this guy?' she demanded, as the path widened into a cobbled lane, lined with pastel pink and sunshine yellow houses nestled together like gingerbread cottages in a child's storybook. 'And if you didn't want me around, why bring me in the first place?'

'To be honest, you're my alibi,' Summer replied apologetically, turning sharply left down a flight of shallow steps connecting the lane with a tiny cobbled square with a fountain in the middle. 'I'm sorry to do this on your first evening but I don't know when I'm going to get another opportunity.'

She nibbled on a hangnail and turned to Caitlin.

'See, I'm not meant to have anything to do with him, and if my father or Ludo knew I was going to meet up with him, they'd – well, just let's say it doesn't bear thinking about.'

She caught Caitlin's anxious expression.

'Listen, I'll explain it all later, OK? Does your mobile work out here?'

Caitlin fished in the pocket of her jeans and glanced at the phone.

'Seems to,' she nodded.

'Great. Don't phone me – if there's any change of plan I'll call you.'

'But—'

'Trust me – all you have to do is go off and have a good time. There's a wicked ice cream place down by the harbour. Meet me back here at six-thirty. Oh, and if anyone asks later, all you say is that you'd forgotten to pack some vital item and I took you to get it. Now, go!'

Caitlin ambled as slowly as she could across the square and down another narrow alleyway, past a faded wooden sign that said *Il porto*, which she took to mean the harbour. Every few seconds she turned, hoping to catch a glimpse of Summer and discover where she was heading, but her friend hadn't moved. She was still standing on the same spot, shielding her eyes from the sun and nodding encouragingly at Caitlin. She knew that until Summer was convinced she was well out of the way, she wouldn't be going anywhere.

Reluctantly she turned into a side street so narrow that she could touch the walls of the houses either side at the same time. Her mind was racing; clearly she'd got the wrong end of the stick. Summer wasn't being stalked – she was a willing participant in something that could be really dangerous. Caitlin knew in that moment that she owed it to her friend – and to Ludo – to find out just what was going on. For a moment, her thoughts turned to that awful story she'd read in *Prego* magazine, the one about the American teenage model who thought her lover was really passionate about her when all the time he was planning to murder her.

As she turned another corner, she spotted a flight of stone steps that led back round to a viewpoint sur-rounded by aloe vera plants and gilly flowers. A small boy with bare feet and tight black curls was squatting down, inspecting what looked like a large toad. Imme-diately her artist's eye saw an opportunity. Running down the steps, she pulled her camera from her bag, checked her light meter, and clicked off a couple of shots before the child caught sight of her, stuck out his tongue and ran off.

Leaning against an iron railing she adjusted the lens and scanned the view before her. Three- and four-storey houses banked up the hillside in higgledy-piggledy terraces, some painted pink, others peach, while a few looked faded and neglected, their less attractive khaki paint peeling in places. Laundry fluttered from makeshift washing lines, anchored to the green-painted shutters or strung across the narrow alleys dividing the houses. Entranced, she took shot after shot, already picturing a collage of prints entitled *Laundry day in Liguria*.

Suddenly, where the houses ended and the olive grove began, she caught a flash of white. She adjusted the focus. It was Summer, weaving her way back past the olive trees and through the lower terraces of the vineyards towards what looked like a ruined church, its crumbling tower sporting a clock-face with just one hand stuck on the figure 5. Zooming in to the maximum that her new, powerful lens would allow, she watched, intrigued, as Summer broke into a run, stumbled for an instant and then disappeared from view.

Clearly the mystery guy was waiting for her in the church. And despite everything Summer had asked of her, Caitlin had no intention of spending the next hour sightseeing.

Not when there was a mystery to be solved and a friend to be saved from herself. And of course, Ludo's eternal gratitude to be won.

Finding her way towards the church was a lot harder than Caitlin had anticipated. For one thing, a lot of the narrow streets were dead ends – she would turn a corner and discover that she had to retrace her steps and start over. For another, the place was beginning to fill up with people – tables were being erected on the cobbles, women were bustling past her, wicker baskets full of fruit and vegetables and a cluster of American tourists blocked the way as they ooh-ed and aah-ed and gee-whizzed over a blackboard advertising walks to the villages of the Cinque Terre.

But eventually, when she'd almost given up hope of getting there, she found herself on a steep stony path, which she could see led directly to the arched doorway of the church. She paused, eyeing up her options. She could hardly march into the church in full view of Summer and her friend and yet she knew it was her duty to make sure that Summer wasn't getting into any danger. Then she noticed that a few metres further on the path forked; the left fork was screened from the church by thick oleander bushes and led round the side of the building. Maybe there would be a window from which she could observe without being seen. She felt her heart begin to beat faster as she scrabbled up the path, slipping from time to time on loose stones and wishing she'd worn trainers instead of her strappy sandals. As she drew closer to the church she slowed down, edging round the building until she came within a metre or so of a narrow, glassless window, almost hidden by russet-coloured creeper. She held her breath and strained to catch any sound from inside the building.

Nothing. Except – yes, just faintly from within the church the low murmur of voices. She was right – that's where they were. She crept closer to the window, stretched out her hand, and as slowly and gently as she could, pulled a tendril of creeper aside in order to peer through into the darkness inside.

What she saw as her eyes adjusted to the gloom made her catch her breath and grab at the broken sill at the base of the window to steady herself.

Summer was sitting on one of the old pews, zipping up a small holdall. Beside her stood a guy, his hand resting lightly on her arm. Despite the dim light inside the old building, it was clear from the way Summer's shoulders were shaking that she was crying.

Caitlin strained her ears to catch what Summer was saying.

'When do we . . . get away . . . take me . . .'

Oh my God, Caitlin thought, clamping her hand to her mouth. They're going to elope!

And as if to reinforce her realisation, as she watched, the guy sat down beside Summer, cupped her face in his hands and kissed her gently. Summer pushed the holdall to one side and laid her head on his shoulder.

'Soon . . .'

She couldn't catch every word that Summer was saying but what she did hear was enough. And one thing was certain: any ideas that Izzy may have had about Summer being afraid of men were clearly way off the mark.

'*Allo moto* . . .' The peace was shattered by the digitalised voice on her mobile phone. '*Allo moto.*'

She grabbed it, heart thumping, and flipped open the cover. Her mother – typical. She switched it off without

{102}

replying and, hardly daring to breathe, remained frozen to the spot, half expecting Summer to burst out of the ruin at any minute, accusing her of spying – which, of course, she was. She pressed herself against the wall of the church and waited.

'What was that? I heard a voice!' Summer's words were now clearly audible. Caitlin spotted a large bush a couple of metres away and hurled herself behind it, wincing as the twigs grazed her legs. Through the tangle of foliage, Caitlin saw the guy – wearing frayed denim shorts and scruffy sneakers – step out of the church and glance round at the terraces. Now that she could see him more clearly, she realised he was quite a bit older than her, short and lean, with olive skin and a mass of short, dark, curly hair.

'You're imagining things, babes,' she heard him say in a broad American accent, as he disappeared back into the building. 'Hey, it's getting late . . . get going . . .' His voice faded as the darkness of the church swallowed him up.

Caitlin's mind raced and she glanced at her watch. She had to hurry – she couldn't risk Summer discovering her up here.

She glanced back at the church door and then ran swiftly to the path behind the cover of the bushes. Her mind was racing; what the hell was going on? Was Summer really going to run away? Was that what she wanted Caitlin to help her with? One thing was clear: she had to act totally innocent and wait for Summer to open up; letting on that she knew anything would be fatal. It might even be a good idea to nip into a shop and buy a few postcards to make it look as if she really had been doing the sightseeing bit.

'Caitlin? Hey – Caitlin!' She jumped and spun round, blinking furiously as the glare of the sinking sun hit her eyeballs.

A familiar figure was waving at her from higher up the lane.

It was Ludo. For a moment, her heart did a double flip at the sight of Ludo's muscular, tanned thighs and bare chest, but then she realised to her horror that he wasn't alone. Judging by the striking family resemblance, the tall guy whose hand was resting on Ludo's shoulder was Sir Magnus Tilney.

This was a disaster. Any minute now, Summer would be leaving the church and Ludo and his dad – if that's who it was – would see her. Worse still, they might even see the guy.

In her mind's eye, the scene played out. Summer screeching that Caitlin had betrayed her, Ludo and the guy getting into a punch-up, Ludo getting hurt, Caitlin mopping his bloodied lip, Sir Magnus banishing his daughter back to England . . .

She had no choice. She turned and hurried up the lane towards them.

'Hi there,' she said, trying to look cool and relaxed despite a scarlet face and perspiring neck.

'Hi – Dad, this is Caitlin Morland, Summer's friend,' Ludo said.

'Good to meet you, Caitlin,' Sir Magnus boomed,

taking her hand and shaking it in a vice-like grip. He was well over six foot, broad-shouldered and with grey hair curling into the nape of his suntanned neck. Dressed in a white, open-necked shirt and tailored shorts, he looked, Caitlin thought, like one of those film stars in the old black and white movies who wore cravats and called their wives 'my dearest dear'.

'But what are you doing all on your own?' he demanded, fanning himself with his straw panama. 'Where's Summer? Don't tell me she's abandoned you already?'

'Oh no, nothing like that, she went to the village,' panted Caitlin, desperately trying to catch her breath, 'She – er – needed something from the shops and I wanted to take photos – the light was perfect and the view's amazing.'

'We can do better than this,' he assured her. 'Wait till you see the Cinque Terre villages from the sea. Now *that* is something worth a couple of reels of film. Though I guess you're all digitalised now, eh?'

He glanced at his watch.

'Good heavens, nearly half-past six. Come on, we'll get back to the house and see what culinary delights await us.'

'No!' Caitlin burst out. 'I mean – thank you, but I promised to meet Summer in the village and she'll wonder where I am.'

'I'll come with you,' Ludo butted in eagerly. 'You go ahead, Dad.'

'Absolutely not!' Sir Magnus declared, ramming his

hat on to his head. He pulled a mobile phone from his pocket and, while Caitlin watched helplessly, punched a number.

'Summer? I don't know what you're up to but get the hell back to the house at once, you understand? You don't go abandoning house guests on their first evening . . . damn! Lost the bloody signal!'

He stuffed the phone back into his pocket and began striding up the hill, muttering under his breath, 'That girl is so like her mother, it scares me sometimes.'

'So – what shall we do tomorrow?' Caitlin could tell by the urgency in Ludo's voice that he was embarrassed by his father's outburst. 'I thought maybe we could take the boat out – if you'd like to, that is.'

'I'd love to,' Caitlin replied, as Ludo's father led them up a narrow flight of stone steps between two cottages.

'Now, that is a good idea,' Sir Magnus butted in, seemingly over his fit of pique. 'Take a picnic, make a day of it – great plan!'

He rubbed his hands together enthusiastically.

'Pity I can't join you, but I've got wine buyers to see. Mind you, Gaby will be tickled pink to go,' he said. 'I'll tell her as soon as we get back.'

Caitlin looked at Ludo, waiting for him to put his father straight; tell him this was just a day for the two of them.

'Right,' Ludo said. 'Fine. Great.'

For a fleeting second, the word 'wimp' shot through Caitlin's consciousness but a half-apologetic shrug of Ludo's shoulders and a silently mouthed 'sorry' quashed it on the spot.

If she had a father like Sir Magnus, she guessed she'd be pretty compliant too.

'Well, thank you so much!'

Caitlin had just finished phoning her mother to assure her that yes, she had arrived safely; yes, she would beware of local romeos, and no, she wasn't going to swim in a sea full of jellyfish, when her bedroom door swung open and Summer stomped in and flung herself down on the end of the bed. 'How could you drop me in it with my father like that?'

'Thanks for knocking,' Caitlin retorted, wrapping a towel tightly round her wet hair and fastening her bathrobe. 'And don't blame me – it wasn't my fault that your dad and Ludo happened to bump into me. What did you want me to do – let them walk right up to the . . .'

She checked herself just in time. As far as Summer knew, Caitlin hadn't a clue what was going on.

'. . . to the village and risk meeting you and this guy strolling around?'

Summer pulled a face and Caitlin noticed that her eyes were suspiciously pink.

'I guess,' she murmured. 'I hadn't thought. Sorry. So, did you have a good time? Where did you go?'

'All over,' Caitlin replied quickly, jettisoning her bathrobe and pulling on her pants and bra. 'I took a few pictures, explored a bit and got lost. What about you? Is everything OK?'

Summer sighed.

'Yes – no – sometimes I wonder if everything will ever be OK again.'

For a moment she fiddled with the corner of the silk throw on Caitlin's bed and then suddenly began talking so fast that Caitlin had trouble keeping up with her.

'He's such a control freak! Well, this time we've got the better of him, and serve him bloody well right! He thinks he can rule everyone's life, make them into something they're not, just to make him feel good . . .'

'But Summer, if he's like that, why the hell are you meeting up with him?' Caitlin gasped, wriggling into a sundress and gesturing to Summer to zip her up.

'Not Alex – my father! Alex is great – he's my total hero. Of course, as far as my dad's concerned the whole di Matteo family are the pits but that's all down to his stupid prejudices.'

Caitlin, reeling from this sudden, uncharacteristic divulgence of information, managed to ask, 'Your father knows him?'

'That's what's so silly about it all. Alex's parents and mine were friends for years – us kids all used to play together. Alex's dad ran this swish restaurant down the coast and he used to let Mum hang her pictures there. It was some arty friend of his that saw them and wanted to do that exhibition I told you about.'

'And that's why your dad and he fell out? Just because your dad didn't want your mum to have this exhibition?'

'I guess,' she sighed. 'He and Mum had these horrendous rows about it, and Mum said she was going to do it anyway – but not long after, she died.'

There was a catch in her voice as she turned away, her fingers brushing her eyes.

'The two families haven't spoken to one another since.'

Caitlin's mind was racing. It was like being caught up in an episode of a TV soap, where no one had shown you anyone else's script. What happened to break the friendship? Why was Summer's father so uptight about his wife's work? Just what was going on between Summer and Alex, and how could she find out about the holdall she'd seen in the church without making her friend suspicious? This was just the kind of story that ended up in magazines like *Prego* and *Spot On*.

'So you can only see him if you meet in secret?' she queried, slipping her feet into flip-flops, her imagination conjuring up the opening paragraph of a *My Secret Love* feature with a soft-focus photo of Summer, the tears on her cheeks digitally enhanced.

Summer nodded. 'It's the pits. See, his family moved back to the States when Alex's granddad died – they're Italian/American and own a chain of restaurants in New England. So instead of being here all through the holidays, Alex only comes for a week or so to visit his other grandparents in Vernazza.'

She smiled suddenly.

'After Mum died I didn't see him for two years because we never came back here. I guess, what with us being in England and the di Matteos in the States, Dad thought he'd cracked it; what he doesn't know is that Alex spent the whole of this last year on a uni exchange – Sussex University, to be exact!'

'In Brighton? So you got to see him . . .' She paused as the pieces of the jigsaw began falling into place.

Summer nodded.

'He rang me last October when he got over there and we met up. That's when we started to – well, you know . . .'

'Fancy one another?'

'Yeah. Big time. Of course, Dad would have gone ballistic, but luckily, he's dead keen on me doing lots of sport – says it's a balance to sitting at the piano all day. So I pretend to go out to play tennis or swim or whatever . . .'

'And see Alex instead! That's why you never went out with the Mulberry Court lot. You were seeing him and using them as an alibi.'

Caitlin eyed her with new respect.

'And Izzy's party!' Caitlin went on. 'You'd been to see him that night, hadn't you? That's why you were in tennis gear, never mind *Wimbledon* – the Movie!'

'Exactly!' Summer replied. 'And that's why I asked you to come out here. It was that history of art class that decided me.'

'Now, you're not making any sense,' Caitlin protested. 'What's *that* got to do with anything?'

'Remember when Mrs Cathcart showed us that picture of *The Three Graces* and you said what you thought was going on?'

'OK, so I lost the plot a bit . . .'

'No, that's the whole point,' Summer stressed. 'You can think out of the box – you see things other people miss. It's like the way you take photos of things that other people don't even notice and how you've just clicked about how me and Alex got to see one another.'

She paused.

'My mum would have liked you,' she said softly. 'Most people just look at a picture, she used to say; only special people know how to search for the message behind it.'

'A bit like that project that Mrs C's given us,' Caitlin said, nodding.

Summer took a deep breath.

'I reckon you and me think like Mum did,' she added, slipping her arm through Caitlin's. 'That's why you're going to help me find out what really went on when Mum died. Why my dad got rid of all her pictures and why my whole family carry on like she's a total unmentionable.'

'Well, Summer my dear, so at last you've brought your friends to see us!' Sir Magnus Tilney put the jug of Pimms he was carrying down on the table and strode across the terrace to greet them, kissing Summer on both cheeks and beaming broadly at everyone. It struck Caitlin that this was a different man from the one who'd blasted his daughter over the phone.

'Now, you, Caitlin, I've met already,' he went on. 'And this is?' He turned to Izzy.

'Izzy Thorpe,' Summer said.

'No relation to that politician fellow? The chap on the world news?' Sir Magnus guffawed. 'The one who's in trouble for enjoying a bit of the highlife . . .'

The colour drained from Izzy's face.

'He's my father, actually,' she replied. 'And he's not—'

'Your father? Oh, don't look so worried, my dear, I'm not criticising the chap. The media, though – that's another matter. Can't trust them further than you can throw 'em – I've had enough run-ins with the press myself to know that.'

He cleared his throat.

'Besides, Parliament's in recess – it'll all blow over. Something of nothing, I don't doubt.'

He turned hastily to Jamie.

'And you are . . .?'

'Jamie Morland, sir, Caitlin's brother.'

'He's my boyfriend,' Izzy butted in, thrusting out her chin in defiance. Caitlin and Summer exchanged amused glances.

'And what do you do, *boyfriend?*' asked Sir Magnus. 'Golf? Tennis?'

'I sail a bit,' Jamie began.

'You're into boats? Wonderful!' Summer's father boomed, clapping Jamie on the shoulder. 'Of course I don't do as much sailing as I used to – broke the bloody collar bone and knackered my hip a year ago, but no doubt I could helm while you crew and . . .'

He grabbed Jamie by the arm and led him away, still talking non-stop.

Caitlin touched Izzy's arm.

'Are you OK?'

'Sure I am,' Izzy snapped. 'What's not to be OK about?'

* * *

Caitlin felt as if she was sitting in the middle of one of those TV adverts for Italian cars or jars of pasta sauce. A long trestle table had been set up under the trees at the side of the villa and was laden with bowls of salad, dishes of olives, baskets of garlic bread and jugs of wine. Two barbecues sizzled away at the side, grilling huge shrimps, whole fish and chicken legs doused in honey and herbs. Sir Magnus had invited friends from the neighbouring villa to the meal, and Caitlin's ears were assailed with the rapid staccato of Italian spoken so fast that she couldn't understand a single word, despite having scanned the pages of *Italian in Seven Days* at the airport. She felt as if any moment now a Fiat Punto would hurtle through the olive groves, or some fat señora would brandish tomato sauce to background music of *Arrivederci Roma* and pronounce that it was full of Italian sunshine for just two pounds thirty-five.

Despite her surroundings, Caitlin was disappointed. She had prayed that Ludo would sit next to her during supper, but he was at the far end of the table next to Katrina, the neighbour's stylish daughter, with whom he was chatting and laughing with far more ease that Caitlin would have wished. She had Izzy on one side and Summer on the other; and since Izzy – who was quaffing Prosecco like it was going out of fashion – had eyes and ears for no one but Jamie, and Summer was jabbering away in fluent Italian to Dino, the neighbour's rather sulky looking son, she spent most of the meal inside her imagination.

She was just dreaming about unmasking the truth

behind the death of Summer's mother and having Ludo hurl himself into her welcoming arms and expressing his lifelong devotion and gratitude, when the sound of gunfire caused her to leap right out of her seat.

'That'll be Freddie, no doubt,' Sir Magnus announced. 'He never could do anything quietly.'

'Or get anywhere on time,' Gabriella muttered under her breath.

The sound of a roaring engine followed by the screeching of tyres on gravel made Caitlin realise that it wasn't gunfire but a motorbike. Already Summer, her dad and Ludo were on their feet, while Gabriella was dabbing her mouth delicately with a napkin and refilling her glass.

'Isn't he just a total dish?' Izzy whispered, pushing back her chair and turning to Caitlin for the first time in an hour. 'Eat your heart out, Johnny Depp!'

Caitlin stared at the guy who was crossing the terrace and waving at everyone. He couldn't have been more different from Ludo; he was tall and muscular, with dark hair brushing his shoulders and a gold earring in his left ear. Caitlin could see what Izzy meant; it was as if one of the Pirates of the Caribbean had landed at Casa Vernazza.

'Hi Ludo, mate, you got here then! How's things?'

He kissed everyone on both cheeks, grabbed a glass and poured a generous slug of Pimms.

'And Summer,' he cried. 'You're looking great – how come my little sister got so grown up in just one term?'

Summer pulled a face at him, and allowed herself to be enveloped in a hug.

'Hi Freddie, remember me?' Izzy had sidled over to him under the pretext of refilling her own glass as everyone settled down again.

Freddie clearly didn't. He opened his mouth, shut it again, looked at her and then glanced at Summer, clearly hoping for help.

'Get real, Izzy,' Summer said. 'He's hardly likely—'

'Izzy! Of course,' Freddie cried, throwing his sister a grateful glance. 'Great to see you again – and you are . . .?'

He turned to Caitlin and Summer introduced her and Jamie.

He was certainly fit, but there was something about him that made Caitlin distinctly uneasy. His eyes were never still – they darted from one person to another, as if sizing up who was the most desirable for him to pay attention to.

'Ludo, let Freddie sit by me,' Sir Magnus ordered. 'There are things we need to talk about. Everyone, eat up – Gaby's special dessert is on its way!'

Caitlin knew she had to act quickly. She nudged Summer on the arm.

'Move – give your seat to Ludo. Please.'

Summer turned, frowning. 'Why?'

'Just do it – you want me to help you, right? So this is pay-back time.'

Summer giggled. 'Oh, I get it! You have got it badly, haven't you? Hey, Ludo! Sit here – I was just going to—'

'Help me with dessert?' Gaby was at her elbow, en route for the house. 'Angel – you can carry the *pannacotta* while I get the peaches.'

Summer followed Gaby, somewhat reluctantly, towards the house and Ludo perched on the chair next to Caitlin.

'This is such a beautiful place,' she began. 'And to think one day it will all be yours . . .'

She stopped, suddenly realising that she sounded like some money-grabbing fortune hunter.

'Not sure I want it,' Ludo murmured. 'Well, not all the hard work with the vineyard and everything. Anyway, that's way ahead. I've got uni first. Now, about tomorrow – I thought we could take *Gina* down the coast, moor off one of the beaches and do a bit of snorkelling?'

Caitlin hesitated. She'd never snorkelled in her life and her swimming was rather like that of a small kitten thrown into a water butt. But to say no would be to kill the romance stone-dead before it started.

'Sounds great!' she enthused as Summer dumped a dish of peaches on the table. 'Ouch!' She winced as the heel of Summer's sandal caught her in the shin.

'Caitlin and I have got plans for tomorrow,' she told her brother firmly. 'We've got this art project to do—'

'We don't have to do it tomorrow,' Caitlin interrupted hastily. 'I mean, we've got ages.'

'Too right,' Ludo said. 'It's the first day of the holidays, for heaven's sake.'

Summer looked decidedly miffed but said nothing.

'Hey, Ludo, did I hear something about a boat trip?' Freddie shouted from across the table. 'That's a cool idea – count me in. Hands up who's for a day on the ocean waves!'

'Me!' Izzy cried, and yanked Jamie's hand into the air. 'And Jamie.'

'Can't you take Dad's boat?' Ludo suggested hastily. 'Mine only really seats six . . .'

'Oh chill, Ludo,' Freddie replied equably, pouring some more wine. 'We'll squash up. It'll be a right laugh.'

'You look exhausted,' Summer said in an unnecessarily loud voice as Caitlin stifled a yawn for the third time in as many minutes. 'Me too. Let's go.'

She hauled Caitlin to her feet.

'We're going to crash,' she announced to the rest of the table. 'See you tomorrow.'

'Thanks for supper,' Caitlin called before Summer dragged her away.

'What did you have to go and do that for?' Caitlin demanded. 'It's only nine-thirty.'

She was shattered, but being dragged away from Ludo was far worse than missing a couple of hours' sleep. Besides, she must have looked so juvenile.

'It's your own fault. I was going to leave this till tomorrow, but there's something I have to show you. And with that lot squiffy and unlikely to move, this is a good time.'

'What is it?'

'Come to my room and you'll see.'

'Lock the door,' Summer ordered, crossing the room and opening a large cupboard.

'That's one of Mum's pictures.' She jerked her head to

the picture above the bed as she dragged a sleeping bag off the top shelf, staggering slightly as though it was really heavy.

'And so are these!' From the sleeping bag she pulled two canvases and laid them side by side. 'What do you think?'

Caitlin gasped. The picture on the wall was of the same scene as the other two – a towering cliff, a pink painted cottage – half derelict and overgrown with weeds – and a huge tree, under which sat the figure of a woman, her face lifted to the sky.

But there the similarity ended. The first picture was perfectly in proportion, and seemed to have been painted on a misty morning; all the colours were soft and muted – the woman's hair was lifting gently as if blown by a breeze and the tree was covered in budding leaves. It was pretty, certainly, but secretly, Caitlin didn't think it was that amazing.

It was the other two pictures that blew her mind.

'Oh, wow!' she breathed, squatting down and looking at them more closely. The colours were vibrant oranges, flame reds, charcoal grey and swathes of purple and indigo. In one, the tree had been made to look grotesque and menacing, its roots exposed as it clung to the cliff edge; the woman's anger was tangible as she clawed at the dark earth with her elongated hands which echoed the shape of the tree roots; the windows of the cottage were shuttered and dark. In the other, the woman dominated the canvas, arms outstretched to the heavens as the wind blew drifts of wet leaves into a river of mud and rainwater; shafts of lightning illuminated her face, on which there was an expression of sheer joy and bliss. And in the corner, the cottage had been reduced to the size and shape of a Monopoly house, its roof sliced as if someone had cut into it like a wedge of cheese, the tiles discarded carelessly around it.

'These are stunning!' Caitlin exclaimed. 'And your mum did all three?'

Summer nodded.

'These are the only ones I managed to rescue,' she said with a sigh. 'Mum used to go away a lot on painting trips and most of her best work was done when she was on her own.'

'What do you mean, rescue?' Caitlin asked.

'Well, she was really generous – she used to give friends pictures as presents – you know, birthdays, Christmas, stuff like that. And she sold quite a few too. When she died, Dad went all peculiar and started buying back the ones she'd sold and even persuaded people to give back their presents.'

'What – you mean he so desperately wanted them all so he could hang them up and remember her?'

'I wish!' Summer almost spat out the words. 'He got them, crated them up and sent them off to be stored somewhere. He gave me this one' – she pointed to the chocolate-box picture – 'as a keepsake. I only got the other two because the owner delivered them to the house while Dad was away on a business trip.'

Suddenly, without warning, she broke into great heaving sobs.

'I miss her so much and I want her back.'

Caitlin put an arm round her shoulders.

'I never even got to say goodbye,' she wept. 'Not properly. It was right at the end of term and I was in America on a school exchange. It was four days before I heard she was dead.'

She wiped her eyes.

'They flew her body back to the UK and so by the time I got home to Brighton, she was all nailed up in the coffin. The boys saw her and put flowers beside her and everything, but I . . .'

She choked on a sob and blew her nose.

'This is the last picture I've got of her.'

She picked up a photograph in a silver frame from her bedside table. It showed a stunningly beautiful woman with dark eyes, golden-blond hair and a generous mouth smiling widely into the camera.

'She's lovely,' Caitlin said.

'Three weeks after I took that, she was dead. She went out for a walk late one night in a thunderstorm and never came home.'

'How come it took your dad so long to reach you?' Caitlin asked.

'He said he didn't want me to miss the chance of playing in the concert at the end of that week,' she replied. 'It was the first time I'd been given a solo spot and he said that he had to think of the living and not the dead.'

Caitlin said nothing as Summer wiped the tears from her cheeks. She had a feeling there was more to come.

'I should never, ever have gone to the States,' she

burst out. 'Mum had always said that when I was around, she felt happy and safe and stuff – she said I was her gift from God, sent to make her happy. She fought Dad tooth and nail to stop me going to boarding school like the boys.'

She blew her nose and looked at Caitlin intently.

'I'll never forgive myself.'

'That's silly,' Caitlin said. 'She must have been so proud—'

'Anyway, the pictures – they are good, aren't they?' Summer broke in swiftly. 'I mean, it's not just my imagination?'

'They're *incredible* – well, at least these two. I'm not so keen on the pretty one.'

'Too ordinary, right?' Summer observed. 'But still good. Look, I'm sorry – I didn't mean to blub. You look pooped.'

She stacked the pictures back in the cupboard as Caitlin, relieved, turned to go.

'Just one more thing,' Summer went on. 'Alex told me today, that he was in Vernazza with his grandparents the other day and there's a new gallery there. He's pretty certain that one of the pictures in the window is Mum's.'

Her face brightened and she grabbed Caitlin's hand.

'Tomorrow we are going there, just you and me.'

'But the boat trip . . .' Caitlin's heart sank but she checked herself, realising that her disappointment was pretty selfish considering what she'd just heard.

'Don't look so worried,' Summer said, smiling. 'We're still going on the trip with the others. But this is the plan . . .'

❧ CHAPTER 6 ❦

*'How many were the examples to justify
even the blackest suspicion?'*
(Jane Austen, *Northanger Abbey*)

CAITLIN RUBBED SUNSCREEN ON TO HER ARMS AND stretched out on *Gina*'s deck.

As they motored along past villages that clung to the hillsides like lopsided cardboard houses in a children's art display, Summer sat beside her, lost in thought, her knees tucked under her chin. Ludo had handed the controls over to Jamie, who had been very enthusiastic at the start, but was now, Caitlin noticed, anxiously looking over his shoulder every few minutes to the back of the boat where Izzy and Freddie were laughing and joking as if they'd known one another for years.

'Who's for a dip?' Gabriella called, pulling off her sarong to reveal a gold and silver tankini. 'Last one in the water's a sissy!'

Jamie killed the engine and she executed a perfect dive, swam under the boat and emerged the other side, laughing and beckoning to them to join her.

Ludo pulled off his T-shirt and dived in beside her.

'Come on, you two,' he called to Caitlin and Summer.

Summer shook her head and waved him away. Caitlin hesitated.

'I can't dive,' she admitted reluctantly. 'And – well, I'm not that strong a swimmer out of my depth.'

She could have kicked herself for being so totally uncool.

'You'll be fine,' Ludo assured her. 'Sit on the edge and slide in. I'll catch you.'

She eased herself gingerly into the cool water, grasping his hand as she did so. As she let go of the boat he caught her and pulled her close and for the briefest instant, their eyes met and his face approached hers, his lips parting slightly.

'*Yow-eeee!*'

A huge splash engulfed them as Freddie dived into the water, closely followed by Izzy, who managed only a cracking belly flop. Caitlin could cheerfully have murdered him. By the time she'd wiped the water from her eyes, Ludo was powering towards the beach, cutting through the water with all the grace and ease of a dolphin. Izzy and Freddie were splashing one another like a pair of hyperactive five-year-olds and Jamie, still at the helm, was starting to look decidedly petulant.

'Bring the boat in, Jamie,' Ludo yelled. 'We can picnic here.' He gestured to a wooden landing stage a hundred metres or so up the beach. Caitlin knew there was no way her uncoordinated breast stroke would get her that far; she pulled herself back on to the deck and sat splashing her feet in the water as they drifted to their anchoring spot.

'Listen,' Summer hissed at her, pulling her to one side. 'As soon as we've eaten, we say we're going for a walk, OK? There's a path from the landing stage that goes round the headland right into Vernazza village.'

Despite wanting to stay as close to Ludo as possible, Caitlin couldn't help feeling a frisson of excitement at the thought of what lay ahead. Those wild paintings by Summer's mum were clearly in a class of their own. It was a crime to have them hidden away from the public. But, she thought, smiling to herself, if her plan took off, Summer's mum wouldn't be a complete unknown for much longer.

And Caitlin Morland would also be celebrated – as the person who brought the work of Elena Cumani-Tilney into the public domain. The art project was just the start.

'It's not there.'

Summer stared disconsolately at the window of La Galleria Lorenzo. None of the four canvases on display bore even the vaguest resemblance to the ones in her bedroom.

'Wait!' Caitlin urged, as Summer turned away. 'Let's go in – they might have changed the window display since Alex saw it.'

Without waiting for a reply, she pushed open the door, ducking under the tendrils of vine trailing over the entrance.

'*Buongiorno, señorita. Benvenuto alla mia galleria piccola.*'
The guy who greeted Caitlin was about her father's age, and twice as large. '*Che cosa posso fare per voi?*'

'Um – *mi dispiace*, but I don't speak Italian,' Caitlin stammered. 'Do you speak English – *parla inglese?*'

'I speak a little, but no very good,' he replied. 'You want picture?'

'I think you have a painting by Elena Cumani-Tilney,' she said.

The guy frowned and eyed her suspiciously.

'You are from the family?' His voice suggested that if this were so, she could leave right there and then.

'Oh, no,' she said innocently, as the bell on the door clanged and Summer peered in and then gingerly entered the shop.

'I'm an art student over from England – oh and this is my friend. Our tutor knows this area well and mentioned the work of this lady and said we should try to see some of it while we were here.'

She paused. 'We thought we saw one of the paintings in the window a couple of days ago.'

The guy nodded slowly.

'Is right,' he said, 'but now – is gone. Sold.'

'Sold?' Summer gasped. 'I don't believe it.'

She hooked her hands behind her neck and banged her elbows together in frustration.

The guy stared at her for a moment and then shrugged.

'But I have more of Elena's work,' the man said. 'You want I bring them?'

'Yes, please!' Summer and Caitlin gasped in unison.

'You wait – they are in the storeroom. By the way, I am Lorenzo Bastellado – I own this gallery.'

'Pleased to meet you,' Caitlin said impatiently.

Within moments Lorenzo was back, carrying two canvases covered in bubble wrap. He laid them on a table in the back corner of the gallery and beckoned them over.

'There is this one,' he said, placing a very small painting of a lemon grove in the conventional, pastel-coloured style on the table. 'And then . . .'

He turned over the second canvas with a flourish.

'There is this one!'

'Oh – that's stunning!' Caitlin cried, her eyes feasting on the exuberant colours and abandoned brush strokes. The painting was of a moonlit sea, jagged rocks and towering cliffs. But the focus of the picture was a rowboat, being tossed on the waves. In the prow of the boat stood a woman and in her arms, lifted high into the air, was a small child. The woman was painted in dark colours but the child was almost luminous in quality – pale, glowing and ethereal like a ghost or spirit.

'Summer, this is amazing,' Caitlin breathed. 'Look at the way the moonlight hits the water . . .'

She turned excitedly to Summer and stopped short.

Tears were pouring down Summer's cheeks and she was shaking from head to toe.

'Summer? What's wrong?' Caitlin looked anxiously at Lorenzo, trying to think of a reason to explain away her friend's tears.

Lorenzo touched Caitlin's arm.

'Let her cry,' he said softly. 'Why not? You also would cry if you see your dear, late mother's work, no?'

'How did you know who I am?' Summer asked a few minutes later when she had managed to compose herself enough to speak.

'That way you banged your elbows,' Lorenzo said, laughing. 'So like your mother – I see that – how you say? – that *gesture*, many times.'

'You knew my mum?' Summer gasped. 'How come?'

Lorenzo sighed.

'Some years ago – maybe three now – I plan to exhibit her pictures in my gallery in Genoa . . .'

'It was you?' Summer exclaimed.

'Ah, but it was not to be.' Lorenzo shrugged. 'Your father – it was felt not, how you say, *appropriate*. He was probably right . . . but a shame.'

Lorenzo's voice trailed off and his tone changed.

'She was so talented, was she not? Such vibrancy . . .'

'But the two styles are so different,' Caitlin observed, glancing from the chocolate box lemon grove to the passion and fire of the seascape.

'It is true,' Lorenzo agreed. 'All her work is good, of course – but the pieces she painted at the abbey – oh! They are, how you say – *meravigliosa!*'

'The abbey?' Summer exclaimed.

Lorenzo frowned.

'You remember – when she have to take time out, to go away, to—'

'Oh, you mean her painting trips! Right – so this abbey was one of the places she went?'

Lorenzo looked away and busied himself with folding up the bubble wrap. 'Sure, that's right.'

'It figures,' Summer said, nodding. 'Loads of her paintings have ruins in – Dad didn't like them, said he preferred houses with roofs on!'

'But I am being rude,' Lorenzo said. 'You would like a drink, yes? Is warm day.'

Summer nodded and Lorenzo disappeared down the stairs.

'Shall I take photos of the pictures?' Caitlin whispered. 'I could blow them up really large . . .'

'Yes, go for it,' Summer urged her. 'Quickly.'

By the time Lorenzo reappeared Caitlin had taken half a dozen shots and was stuffing her camera back in its case.

Lorenzo tossed a can of lemonade at each of them. As she yanked at the ring-pull, Caitlin noticed Summer's hands were shaking.

'What was the other picture? The one that was sold?' Summer asked.

'This is it.' He laughed, pointing to the painting of the moonlit sea. 'When I had to sell it, I realise I cannot part with it. And now I know why – you must have it. It is only right.'

He gazed at the picture for a long time.

'Your mother, she gave it to me as gift,' he explained. 'But I feel it is right for it to go to you.'

He walked briskly over to a cabinet and pulled out some fresh bubble wrap.

'I can't take it with me now,' Summer said. 'My father . . . well, will you keep it for me?'

'Of course,' Lorenzo replied. 'And at home, I have something else you might like. I will make sure you get it.'

'You want my address?'

'I know your address,' he said laughing. 'Everyone know the Tilneys of Casa Vernazza, no? I will have it delivered, OK?'

'*Allo moto, allo moto!*' Caitlin's phoned blared, shattering the peace of the gallery.

'Yes? Oh, hi Ludo. Er – no, no we're on our way back – what? Oh, OK then. Hang on.'

She pulled a face at Summer, who was staring at her open-mouthed.

'It's Ludo for you,' she said. 'He tried your phone but it's off. Izzy gave him my number – sorry.'

Summer snatched the phone from Caitlin's hand.

'We're coming, OK? Like what's the rush? Oh well, I might have guessed it would be her. Caitlin's just sketching something and then we'll come.'

She thrust the phone back into Caitlin's hand and turned to Lorenzo.

'I'll be back for the painting just as soon as I can, OK? And thanks, thanks so much.'

Summer was walking so quickly that Caitlin could hardly keep pace with her.

'Isn't it brilliant that you're getting the picture?' she said. 'When are we going to be able to come back for it?'

'We? Get real! From now on it's just me – not you. I thought I could trust you.'

'What?' Caitlin demanded. 'You can! What have I done? It's not my fault Ludo got hold of my number.'

'It's a good thing he did,' Summer retorted. 'The moment I heard that stupid ring tone, I knew I'd heard it before. You followed me last night, didn't you?'

'No, I didn't,' Caitlin stammered, cursing herself for not changing the ring tone.

'Don't lie,' Summer snapped. 'There's hardly likely to be anyone else with such a naff ring tone. So what were you doing? Spying and planning on running back to tell tales?'

This, Caitlin thought hurriedly, called for what her father called 'a damage limitation exercise'. She could admit to everything and risk Summer clamming up and shutting her out totally, or she could lie just a little bit and hopefully be in with a chance of unravelling the whole mystery.

'Summer, I don't know what you're on about,' she said firmly. 'The only time my phone's rung since I've been here is when I went for a walk up the hill behind the village. My mum rang to check I'd arrived – like how overprotective is that? If you heard that, you were either sitting in a bush . . . hey, you weren't – you know – *doing stuff* with that guy . . .?'

Her comment had the desired effect.

'Get real!' Summer retorted. 'Go on. What else did you do?'

'And I took some pictures near that old church – and that's it! So that's where you were, right?'

Summer nodded, pausing as they turned on to the cliff path and saw the others in the distance, loading stuff back on to the boat.

'And you didn't see anything?'

'What was there to see?' Caitlin asked as casually as she could. 'Like I said, I was too busy taking pictures.'

'OK, sorry.' Summer looked mildly abashed. 'Anyway, we'd better get back to the boat; apparently Gabriella's got one of her headaches.'

Caitlin said a silent prayer of thanks for her narrow escape.

'I said you'd been sketching,' Summer called over her shoulder. 'What if they ask to see your work?'

'That's the least of our problems,' Caitlin replied. 'Don't worry – I'll deal with it. And before you ask – no, I won't be telling anybody about anything we've done today, OK?'

Summer nodded. 'You'd better not,' she said. 'I'm still not convinced you're being straight with me.'

'Why wouldn't I be?' Caitlin asked. 'What's not to be straight about?'

Caitlin tried to ignore the stab of conscience as she smiled reassuringly at Summer. The lie was, after all, in a very good cause. And one day, Summer would thank her.

It was well past midnight and Caitlin couldn't sleep. The more she thought about it, the more determined she was to put the plan she had devised that morning into practice. She had intended to confide in Summer but now she wasn't so sure.

All the way home in the boat that afternoon, Summer had sat in the stern, her back resolutely turned on Caitlin, yabbering away to Freddie, Izzy and Jamie in an artificially bright voice. Gabriella had gone below to lie down and Caitlin had Ludo all to herself, which was great – except for the questions. He'd clearly had a few beers over lunch and there was a can at his side as he steered *Gina* homewards. Now, Caitlin lay on the bed, running and re-running their extraordinary conversation in her mind.

'So, where did you two go?' Ludo had asked the moment they got under way. 'What did you draw? Can I see?'

That last question she had been ready for.

'Not yet – it's just rough sketches and I have this thing: no one sees my stuff till it's finished. I know it sounds precious but . . .'

'No, that's OK, Mum was just the same. She'd never show us a thing till she thought it was perfect.'

He had suddenly looked so young and so downcast that Caitlin's heart lurched. Maybe, she had thought, now was the moment to get him to open up a bit more.

'Your mum's stuff was amazing.' She had caught her breath as Ludo turned sharply and stared at her.

'I mean, I *guess* it was, not that I'd know,' Caitlin had said. 'Just from what Summer said about her talent. And the picture on her wall.'

'Does Summer talk about Mum a lot?' This was one question Caitlin hadn't been prepared for. She had hesitated, not knowing what she was expected to say.

'Well, she never used to say anything about her, but the last couple of days – well, yes, quite a lot actually. She really misses her.'

'We all do, but the thing is . . .' He had dropped his voice, even though the throbbing of the boat's engine made it impossible for anyone else to hear. '. . . the rest of us started missing her years before she died.'

Caitlin had wondered just how many cans of beer he'd consumed.

'What do you mean?'

'Oh – I just meant, you know, Freddie and me, being sent off to boarding school – well, we got used to not having Mum.'

He had eased the throttle on the boat and turned her towards the harbour.

'Lucky for Summer then, getting to stay at home,' Caitlin had commented. 'She said her old school was just round the corner from your house in Brighton.'

Ludo had nodded. His knuckles were turning white as he gripped the steering wheel.

'Yeah. She was Mum's favourite, no doubt about that. Poor little sod. If it hadn't been for Gaby coming over and moving in to—'

'Did I hear my name?' Gaby had emerged from the galley, looking slightly less pale than before.

'Oh, hi! I was just saying to Caitlin that she should go and check you were OK,' Ludo had blustered. 'Only five minutes and we'll be back.'

'Great,' Gaby had replied. 'I'll just get my things.'

With that she had disappeared down the hold again.

Caitlin was struggling to get her head around all this new information and was on the point of pressing Ludo for an explanation when Jamie had come over and plonked himself down beside them.

'Hi, mate – you OK?' Ludo had asked. 'Want to take her in?'

'Sure, thanks,' Jamie had replied eagerly, edging over and taking the wheel. 'By the way, is your brother here for long?'

'Rest of the summer, I guess – till uni starts. Why?'

'No reason.' Jamie had sighed. 'Just wondered.'

For a moment now, lying on the bed and trying to keep cool by flapping the sheet up and down over her sweating body, her thoughts strayed to Jamie's question. She had a nasty feeling that it had a great deal to do with the way Freddie and Izzy had been thick as thieves all day, or the way Freddie muscled in on every conversation and worse, the way Izzy let him.

She'd have to sort her brother out in the morning, tell him to be more assertive. She couldn't help wondering whether Summer had been right when she'd said that Izzy made mincemeat of any guy who fancied her.

Thinking of Summer brought her thoughts sharply back to the mystery of the Tilney family. Because a mystery it certainly was. Why would Ludo call Summer a poor little sod, when she got to stay at home with her mum? And more importantly, why would Gabriella leave Italy and move in to a marital home unless she was out for one thing and one thing only? To break up a marriage and – no! Surely not. She couldn't – but if Sir Magnus was in on it too, she could.

Gabriella and Magnus could have *murdered* Summer's mum and then pretended it was an accident. Her mind began racing.

'Oh my God!'

What was it Summer had told her? That her mum felt safe and happy when she was around – so could that mean that Summer's mum knew, deep down, that her life was in danger, and that even Sir Magnus wouldn't do anything while his own daughter was on the scene? Summer's school trip to the States would have given him and Gaby the perfect opportunity. And Summer had admitted that it had taken her father four whole days to let her know that her mother was dead. Four days spent covering up their tracks, perhaps.

Caitlin's heart began racing and she was off the bed, pacing the room now, overwhelmed by the thoughts chasing each other round and round in her head. She would have to talk to Summer, make her see that she was on her side. And then she'd have to start putting her plan into action. She had the perfect alibi. The whole family knew that she had an art project to complete.

What they *didn't* know was that the paintings and the life – and death – of Elena Cumani-Tilney, was going to be the topic.

❧ CHAPTER 7 ❧

'A woman in love with one man cannot flirt with another.'
(Jane Austen, *Northanger Abbey*)

'SUMMER, CAN I COME IN?' CAITLIN CALLED THROUGH THE keyhole of Summer's bedroom the following morning before breakfast.

The door opened and Summer, her hair still tousled from sleep, waved her in.

'What's the matter? Are you OK? You look a bit sunburnt,' she said, sleepily.

'I'm fine, but listen – I've been thinking. You want to find out the truth about your mum and all this mystery, right?'

Summer yawned and nodded.

'And you want me to help?'

Summer nodded again.

'Right – so the first thing you have to do is to be really nice to Gabriella for a bit – I mean, seriously matey.'

'Are you out of your mind?' Summer exploded. 'After what she did to my mum?'

'What do you mean?'

'She made that last year of her life a misery,' Summer declared. 'Taking over, bossing everyone about – Mum said that she was killing her creativity. She had to keep going away in order to paint at all.'

'Was this – I mean, did she live with you? In England?' She wasn't sure that she should let on about her conversation with Ludo, given Summer's somewhat volatile nature.

'Off and on,' Summer grunted. 'She used to be Mum's best friend, way back – she had this house in the next village. Well, she's still got it but she rents it out to holidaymakers now she's shacked up with Dad. She used to come to stay with us in Brighton from time to time and when we were over here, she was always hanging around.'

She glared at Caitlin.

'So, who put you up to this dumb idea about sucking up to her? My dad? Ludo the goody-goody? I don't believe you, Caitlin – I thought you were on my side.'

'I am, and no one put me up to it,' Caitlin retorted. 'I do have a brain of my own you know, and if you used yours, you might see what I'm getting at.'

'Go on,' Summer muttered.

'I don't want to upset you,' Caitlin began, 'but what if your dad wanted to get rid of all her pictures because – well, because . . .'

'Get on with it!'

'Because he didn't want to be reminded that he'd already got rid of her?'

Summer stared at her.

'You mean . . .?'

'If Gabriella and your dad were an item, then perhaps—'

'Shut up! Shut up! SHUT THE HELL UP!'

Caitlin froze. Summer had picked up a book from her bedside table and hurled it across the room, hitting the make-up bottles on her dressing table and sending them flying.

'Summer, don't!' Caitlin gasped. 'I might not be right, it was just a thought, and you did ask . . .'

'So go on, say it,' Summer shouted at her. 'Say what you're really thinking.'

'I just did,' Caitlin ventured nervously.

'And the rest,' Summer urged, her voice rising in anger. 'Say that it's my fault, that if I hadn't begged and begged to go to America that Easter, Mum would be alive and . . .'

The rest of her words were lost in choking sobs.

'Summer, that's crazy – *of course* it wasn't your fault! That's not what I meant. It was just that when Ludo said about Gabriella moving in—'

'Oh, so you've been talking to Ludo as well, have you? So much for keeping confidences!'

'Summer, listen! He started talking to me, right?'

'And said that Gabriella moved in because I couldn't look after Mum properly, right? Because Dad said things were falling apart? That I was just a kid and couldn't cope? That so wasn't true – just because none of them understood her artistic temperament . . .'

'Why should you have to look after her?' Caitlin burst out. 'Was she sick?'

{138}

'You are so unreal! Get out of my room – get out! Now!'

'Have you and Summer had a falling out?' Izzy flopped down beside Caitlin at the edge of the pool, where Caitlin had just put in a couple of lengths before breakfast. 'I heard shouting and she's in a right strop – just pushed past me without so much as a "hello",' Izzy continued.

'There's something really odd going on,' Caitlin replied thoughtfully. 'Does Freddie ever talk about his mum?'

'Not really,' Izzy replied. 'The only time he mentioned her was when he said that he was fed up with his family being so straight-laced and that he intended to live life in the fast lane, because you never knew when you'd end up like his mum – dead and disgraced.'

'Disgraced? Did he really say that?'

'Yeah – I thought it a bit odd at the time. But I always told you there was more to the whole story than we knew.'

'What I think—' Caitlin began.

'Tell me later,' Izzy blurted out, gesturing to Jamie, who was ambling out of the house and heading their way. 'Right now, I need your help. You have to sort Jamie out.'

'Jamie? Don't tell me you two have had a row?'

'Not yet, but we sure as hell will if he doesn't loosen up,' Izzy retorted. 'He's so possessive – every time I talk to Freddie or go skinny dipping—'

'*Skinny dipping?*'

'Oh, don't look at me like that!' Izzy replied. 'Jamie could've come too – not my fault he's so uptight. Last night after you'd gone to bed we went down to the beach – it was so cool. But Jamie just sulked – I mean, is that juvenile or what?'

'That's a bit unfair,' Caitlin protested. 'I mean, you *are* his girlfriend, not Freddie's – I guess he just wants more time with you on your own. I thought that's what you wanted too.'

'Sure.' Izzy shrugged. 'But you've seen what Freddie's like – he's all over me. I've tried ignoring him . . .'

'Oh yeah? And I've tried deep-sea diving in a teacup. Come off it, Izzy. The bottom line is you're a grade one flirt.'

Izzy pulled a face.

'I'm just naturally gregarious, that's all,' she explained. 'Anyway, if Jamie thinks he owns me, he's wrong. No one does, because I'm a free spirit – and he'd better get that into his head right now.'

She turned to Caitlin, lips pouted.

'But I hate arguing with him, because he is cute,' she said smiling fondly. 'And he's got the sexiest body.'

'Oh puh-leese,' Caitlin sighed.

'So – could you like talk to him? Get him to see things my way? Say it didn't mean anything – just a bit of fun?'

'I'll have a word,' Caitlin said noncommittally. A word of warning, she thought. If he wanted Izzy he'd need to stop being quite so patient and nice.

* * *

'Sorry,' Summer murmured, grabbing a panini and some cheese from the kitchen table. 'I didn't mean to go off on one.'

'Whether you mean it or not, you keep doing it,' Caitlin snapped, partly because she was still angry and partly because PMT was kicking in big time. 'You said you wanted my help, you talk about being glad that I can think out of the box, and then when I do, you go ballistic.'

She poured some orange juice and piled her breakfast plate with rolls and jam. Hormones made her very hungry.

'I know,' Summer sighed. 'It's just that I feel guilty and then I get cross with myself and take it out on the nearest person.'

'But that's what I don't get,' Caitlin stressed, pausing in the doorway to avoid being overhead by the rest of the family, who were already gathered round the table. 'What's for you to feel guilty about?'

'If you're right, and if Gabriella and Dad had a thing going, then I shouldn't have gone away – because if I'd been there, nothing could have gone on, could it?'

'Oh, get real,' Caitlin replied. 'What do you do when you want to see Alex? You find a way. Just because they're old, doesn't mean they can't do the same thing.'

'Please, don't make me think about the details,' groaned Summer.

'Besides,' Caitlin continued, 'you said Gaby has a house of her own – they could have gone there any time, whether you were around or not.'

Summer nodded slowly.

'I hadn't thought about that. I guess seeing Mum's painting of that boat yesterday freaked me more than I realised. I remembered the night she took me out.'

'You mean it was a *real event*? She didn't make it up?'

Summer shook her head.

'I was really little,' she said softly. 'Mum woke me up and said she wanted to show me the stars. We got into the rowing boat – my granddad was alive then and it was his – and she rowed out really far and it was quite rough. I was – well, a bit scared.'

'I'm not surprised,' Caitlin remarked.

'Then suddenly, she stopped rowing and picked me and held me right up as high as she could. And she sang some funny song – and I remember screaming.'

'That's well weird,' Caitlin gasped.

'No, it's not!' Summer's expression changed completely. 'You sound just like Dad when you say things like that! I only cried because I was a kid – it was just Mum being Mum. She did things like that and OK, sometimes she was bit silly, but then all artists are a bit quirky.'

She pulled a face at Caitlin.

'Even you throw water over yourself at parties,' she muttered.

Caitlin laughed, thankful that Summer seemed less touchy.

'True,' she agreed. 'Mad or what?'

'So, what's with this plan about me being nice to Gabriella?' Summer asked. 'You'd better have a pretty good reason.'

'We need to soften her up, right?' Caitlin explained.

'People always let things slip when they feel safe. Can't you ask her a few leading questions? Maybe she knows why your dad is so against Alex's family.'

'You reckon?'

Caitlin saw she had got Summer on-side.

'Must do – and the easiest way to find out is for you to be all over her. She's desperate for you to like her.'

She jerked her head in the direction of the terrace. 'And here's your chance,' she said with a smile. 'Just do it – pretend it's a drama workshop or something!'

'Surprise!' Gaby cried, as the girls sat down at the table with their breakfast plates. 'I was just telling the others – I've booked us a table for lunch at the Splendido in Portofino! My treat!'

'Oh wow!' Summer cried, turning to Caitlin. 'The Splendido is the best people-watching place on earth – all the movie stars go there. And the food is heaven!'

'So you'll come?' Gaby asked. 'I thought us girls could spend the morning in a little light retail therapy and then meet up with the guys for lunch.'

'Oh, Gaby, that's a brill idea!' Summer jumped up and gave her a hug. 'You're a star!'

Gabriella looked stunned but delighted. Ludo and Sir Magnus glanced at one another and then at Caitlin, and broke into broad grins.

'Well now, Jamie,' Sir Magnus began, 'what do you say to joining me on my catamaran? Much more fun sailing than hanging around while the girls spend my money, eh?'

'Great, I'd love to,' Jamie said.

'Of course, probably a good idea if you come too, Ludo – and Freddie. Tricky berthing at Portofino, as I recall. Where *is* Freddie, by the way?'

'Haven't a clue. In bed, probably,' Ludo replied, 'judging by the amount he drank last night.'

'No, he's gone out,' Izzy informed them. 'To Genoa. He won't be back for ages.'

Six pairs of eyes fixed on her face.

'Don't know why,' she went on hastily. 'Guys, eh? So unpredictable, aren't they?'

She is up to something, Caitlin thought. I've seen that oh-so-innocent look before – and it doesn't fool me.

'Summer, look!'

Caitlin nudged her friend as they waited for Izzy, who was gazing into a shop window full of Armani and Missoni outfits with price tags like telephone numbers.

'See this?' She thrust a postcard into Summer's hand. 'Look on the back.'

'Sunset at the Abbey of San Fruttuoso,' Summer read. 'So what— oh! The abbey! You think that's where Mum went to paint?'

'Could be,' Caitlin agreed. 'It would be cool to check it out.'

She turned to the street vendor who was selling the postcards.

'How do we get to this abbey?' she asked.

'Is about two hour walk,' he said in broken English.

'But there is boat from harbour – not so long. Is very beautiful.'

'We can't go,' Summer reminded her. 'Lunch is in half an hour.'

'Don't worry, I've got an idea,' Caitlin said. 'Leave it to me.'

This I could get used to, thought Caitlin, savouring her *pansoti* with herb and nut sauce and sipping crisp Ligurian white wine that made her palate tingle and her confidence soar. They were sitting on the terrace of the hotel, overlooking the cerulean blue sea dotted with yachts leaning into the breeze that skimmed the tops of the myrtle bushes below them. Sir Magnus was talking nineteen to the dozen to Ludo, and Jamie was, by the look on Izzy's face, playing footsie with her under the table.

She surreptitiously kicked Summer and turned to Gabriella.

'This is *so* kind of you,' she said, in her best thanking-great-aunts voice. 'I'm really enjoying myself.'

'You're more than welcome,' Gaby replied with a smile. 'We want you to have as many lovely experiences as possible while you are here.'

'Well,' Caitlin said, 'Summer and I were wondering about exploring the abbey.'

The expression on Gaby's faced changed instantly. The smile faded and she stared first at Caitlin, then across the table at Sir Magnus, who clearly hadn't heard a word, and then back to Caitlin again.

'The abbey? What abbey?'

I'm on to something here, Caitlin thought with excitement, giving Summer another little kick.

'This one,' Caitlin said, handing Gabriella the postcard.

'Oh! That abbey. What about it?'

'I'd love to go there and paint it,' Caitlin said. 'I really must get started on my art project.'

'Me too,' Summer said. 'We've got to find a work of art and then do a whole portfolio of stuff about it . . .'

'Well, you won't find any paintings at the abbey,' Gabriella replied. 'No point wasting your time there. Now, how about tomorrow I take you to Genoa? Plenty of art there for you to soak up.'

She's changing the subject, Caitlin thought, glancing at Summer. She doesn't want us at the abbey. Now, all we have to do is find out why.

'Not tomorrow—' Summer began and then stopped as her mobile shrilled, to which the diners at the neighbouring table responded by giving her a withering look.

'Summer!' her father exploded. 'You know full well this is a phone-free zone. Switch the damn thing off. Now!'

'It was Alex trying to reach me,' Summer whispered to Caitlin in the ladies' loo. 'Look, can you go and keep Gabriella occupied while I phone him back?'

'Sure,' Caitlin said, nodding. 'Mind you, if she needs a wee, I can hardly tell her she's not allowed.'

'Just come in talking loudly, OK? I'll lock myself in a cubicle. Now, go!'

Caitlin wandered slowly through the luxurious hotel, with its black and white marble floors and amazing *trompe l'oeil* paintings on the pale pink walls, and pretended she was a 1930s film star, heading for an assignation with her secret lover. As if fate were on her side, as she walked through to the terrace she caught sight of Ludo halfway down the steps to the swimming pool, deep in conversation with his father and Gabriella.

She leaned over the stone balustrade, praying that he would look up and catch her eye, and imagined him springing back up the steps two at a time, sweeping her into his arms, tipping her chin, bringing his lips down on hers . . .

'When she asked about the abbey, I nearly had a fit!' Gabriella's voice wafted up to her on the breeze. 'Thank the Lord it was the wrong abbey!'

She turned and her next words were lost to Caitlin. But then Ludo spoke, his voice rising with each word.

'God how I hate all this secrecy! Sometimes I feel like telling Summer the truth myself. She's got a right to know.'

'Ludo, no! Please . . .' Magnus broke in. 'We agreed – it's best left alone.'

'That's all very well, but what if someone else . . .' Ludo replied, as Caitlin strained to catch his words. 'I have a feeling that Alex di Matteo . . . evening when I was . . . can't blame . . . stupid . . . if he said . . .'

A waiter walked past and dropped a stainless steel

dish cover on to the flagstones. Ludo and Sir Magnus turned and Caitlin knew she'd been seen. She was glad she had had the foresight to put her sunglasses on. Ludo waved and she pretended not to see. It wasn't until he called her name that she turned and ran down the steps.

'Oh, hi!' she said. 'Sorry – didn't see you. I was miles away.'

It wasn't a lie, she told herself. Her mind was full of her next move. She had to find out which abbey was causing Gabriella so much angst. More importantly, she had to find out just what Ludo knew about Alex. And she had to warn Summer that her secret could be blown any second.

She knew it was probably wrong to feel this way, but unravelling this mystery was one of the most exciting things she'd ever done.

'Look, you two, do you mind if I just call in at my place on the way home?' Gabriella asked, negotiating the narrow street out of Portofino. 'I want to check on the new tenants – they had a funny look about them.'

Izzy had gone on the boat with the guys – no surprise there, Caitlin thought – and she and Summer were sitting in the back of Gabriella's car, half asleep with the effects of wine and sunshine.

'Sure, fine,' yawned Summer. 'Whatever.'

Caitlin felt her eyes closing as the car twisted and turned its way up the hillside. She must have nodded off, because the slamming of the driver's door woke her with a jolt.

'Sorry,' Gaby mouthed to Caitlin, gesturing at Summer who was sound asleep. 'That's my house over there. I'll only be five minutes.'

She waved and began walking up the flower-lined pathway to the house. Caitlin stared. The house was painted pink. It had a tiled roof. And there was a tree in front of the cottage, a tree that clung to the cliff edge with its roots exposed.

A tree just like the one in Elena's paintings.

Within seconds, she had decided what to do. She glanced at the still-sleeping Summer, and gently opened the car door. Whipping her camera out of its case, she fired off a whole load of shots, some of the cottage, some of the tree and several of the view.

'If they're any good, I'll buy one for my website,' Gaby laughed as she left the house and walked down the path towards Caitlin. 'It needs updating. Mind you, so does the house!'

'It's such a beautiful place,' Caitlin enthused. 'No wonder Summer's mum liked to paint it.'

'*What*? Oh, the picture in Summer's room, Yes, that's this place. Elena used to come here a lot – we were friends for years, you know.'

'Summer said there were loads more paintings by her, but they're all in store,' Caitlin remarked innocently. 'Why's that?'

'I – well, I suppose Magnus thought they might deteriorate. A lot of them, I understand, weren't framed – and besides, it's upsetting to have too many reminders . . .'

She was clearly out of her depth.

'It must have been awful, her dying like that. So were you here when she died?'

'What? No. I was away. Now then, we must get going. Oh, look, Summer's awake. Let's change the subject, shall we?'

It was late afternoon before Caitlin and Summer were alone. The moment Izzy arrived back at the villa she had gone off with the newly returned Freddie, which meant they first had to get rid of Jamie, who was mooching around by the pool, looking disconsolate.

'Just tell her you won't tolerate it,' Caitlin had suggested, after Summer had slipped away to practise her flute in the gazebo. 'It's no good dripping about here – if you want her, *assert* yourself.'

'You're right, I'll do it,' Jamie had declared. 'I'll tell her she has to choose – him, or me.'

'That's more like it,' Caitlin had replied encouragingly. 'Find out where you stand once and for all.'

'I've got it,' Summer said excitedly, the moment she and Caitlin had some space to themselves.

'Got what?'

'The parcel from Lorenzo,' she explained. 'He left it with Luigi at the gatehouse. It's a sketchpad with some pencil drawings of Mum's. I've hidden it in my room – I'll show you later.'

She stretched out on the sunbed and yawned.

'What about this abbey?' she mused. 'Do you reckon we should try to go there? I don't see what it's going to tell us.'

Caitlin shook her head and decided that she'd had enough of keeping things to herself. She told Summer what she'd heard Gabriella saying that afternoon at the hotel.

'So there *is* an abbey, and she doesn't want us to know about it,' Caitlin concluded. 'Have you got a computer?'

'There's one in Dad's study, but no one is allowed near that, and Ludo's got a laptop – but don't change the subject!'

'I'm not – I want to go on the internet, find out all the abbeys around here and see if – well, I'm not sure what I want to see, but it's worth a go.'

'OK – you could borrow Ludo's and say that you're researching for the project,' Summer agreed. 'I'll ask him.'

'And there's something else,' Caitlin said. 'You never told me that the cottage in your mum's pictures was Gaby's.'

'Is it?' Summer looked amazed. 'How do you know?'

'I used my eyes, silly – the tree on the edge of that cliff gives it away. OK, so she's used artistic licence by making the cottage derelict and spooky – but then, maybe that was how she wanted it to be. Kind of depicting that anything that belonged to Gaby had to be destroyed – or like Gaby was destroying her life?'

Summer's mouth dropped open. 'Wow! I've seen that cottage a dozen times and it never clicked.'

'I took photos of it because I've got this idea.'

She touched Summer's arm. 'You want your mum's work recognised, right? You want your dad to realise that locking it all away is a crime.'

'Exactly,' Summer said. 'Not that there's any chance of that happening.'

'Isn't there? What if I make one of your mum's paintings the subject of my project? Do what Mrs Cathcart said, and find out the story behind the picture and then make sure your father sees what I've done before I go home?'

Summer stared at her.

'He'd go ballistic – he'd throw a total wobbly.'

'He couldn't actually do anything,' Caitlin reasoned. 'I'm a guest – and after all, I would have simply been innocently working on a painting I saw in a shop window, wouldn't I?'

Summer chewed her bottom lip and then beamed at Caitlin.

'Do it,' she urged. 'After all, what have we got to lose?'

'I'll need a photo shop with a machine for printing digital pictures,' Caitlin murmured as they walked upstairs to shower before supper.

'There's one in the pharmacy,' Summer told her. 'I'll show you tomorrow. But right now – I've got a favour to ask you.'

'Go on.'

'That phone call from Alex – his gran wants him to take her to Milan for a week to see her sister, and they're leaving in a couple of days,' she said. 'It's awful – I just simply *have* to see him before he goes. We've got stuff to sort. Can you cover for me?'

'What? Come with you and hang around like before?'

Caitlin didn't mean to sound petulant but the prospect wasn't exactly exciting. And perhaps this was the moment to warn her that Ludo might well be on her trail.

'No, nothing like that,' Summer said eagerly. 'We're meeting tonight – eleven o'clock. You don't need to know more than that.'

'Eleven o'clock? Why so late?'

'And you say it's *me* that doesn't use my brain! Like I'm really going to march off in broad daylight and risk being seen.'

She lowered her voice. 'After supper, I'm going to say I've got a migraine coming on – I get them sometimes. They'll think I've gone to bed and I'll be free to slip out and meet Alex. Cool, eh?'

'You can't go on with all this cloak and dagger stuff for ever, you know,' Caitlin reasoned. 'Can't you talk to your dad? I mean, whatever argument he had with Alex's family shouldn't be allowed to affect your life.'

'This presupposes my father is a reasonable man. But don't worry, this will be sorted very soon. They won't know what's hit them.'

'Summer – what—'

'The less you know, the less you can be blamed, OK? Trust me – I know what I'm doing.'

She looked so excited that Caitlin didn't have the heart to ruin it. She knew how she would feel if she was having a secret assignation in the dark with Ludo.

She sighed. The way things were going, that was never going to happen.

'So where's this sketch pad, then?' she asked. 'You said you'd show me.'

Summer beckoned her into her room, opened a drawer, removed a pile of clothes and tossed it at her. Caitlin began flicking through the pages of pencil sketches – more seascapes, more forked lightning, a brilliant self portrait, a picture of an old building . . .

'Hey, Summer, look at this one.'

She stabbed the page with her finger.

'Mm, nice,' Summer murmured, wriggling out of her shorts.

'*Mm, nice,*' mimicked Caitlin. 'Look what it says in the bottom corner!'

Summer peered over her shoulder.

'*The Abbey, July 2004,*' she read. 'So that's it – that's where she went to paint!'

'So,' Caitlin went on excitedly, 'we look on the internet, and find the abbey that looks like this one – and then we'll know exactly where she went. Can I hang on to this? In case I get a chance to ask Ludo for the laptop?'

'Sure,' Summer said, looking at herself in the mirror. 'Do you think my legs are getting any browner?'

'But you've only just got here!' Gabriella gasped over supper, when Izzy announced, quite cheerfully it seemed to Caitlin, that she and Jamie would be leaving in two days' time.

'It's been amazing and I'm really grateful,' Izzy declared, slipping her arm through Jamie's. 'But Jamie

{154}

says he'll take me to Venice, and I've *always* wanted to go there . . . isn't he a honey?'

She planted a kiss on Jamie's cheek and Caitlin heaved a sigh of relief. She'd finally managed to get her brother back on track.

Caitlin had just climbed into bed when there was a knock on her bedroom door.

'Who is it?'

She prayed it wasn't Gabriella or Ludo, hunting for Summer. She'd done the dying swan bit with the migraine so well that they were all probably frightened she was going to expire at any minute.

'It's me – Jamie. Can I come in?'

'Sure, it's unlocked.'

The moment she saw her brother's face, she knew something was wrong.

'It's Izzy. She's gone.'

'*Gone?*'

'With that slimeball Freddie!' he stormed. 'I don't believe this – all through supper he was going on and on about his bloody motorbike and how much it cost and how fast it could go. And then she said—'

'Let me guess,' Caitlin interjected. 'She said she'd always wanted to go on the back of a motorbike.'

'How did you know? You didn't put her up to it, did you?'

'Give me credit for some sense,' she sighed. 'It's just that – well, that's the way Izzy operates, I'm afraid.'

'Now, don't you start slagging her off,' Jamie replied

defensively. 'It's not *her* fault – she was just being friendly. But now they've gone for what Freddie calls a burn-up down the coast road.'

He perched on the end of Caitlin's bed.

'You don't think she's falling for Freddie, do you?'

He looked so crestfallen and embarrassed that she didn't have the heart to tell him what she really thought.

'No, of course not,' she replied. 'And anyway, after tomorrow you'll be on your own with her, won't you? That idea of yours about Venice was ace – can you afford it?'

'It was her idea, not mine,' he admitted. 'But at least I get her to myself and even if it takes my last hundred quid to do it, so what? She's worth it.'

I'm not so sure about that, thought Caitlin.

'We need a plan,' she told him firmly.

'A plan about what?'

'If Mum or Dad phone to speak to you, I'll say you're in the pool and then I'll text you on your mobile and you can call them back. That way, they'll never know where you are.'

'Do you know, I would never have thought of that?' Jamie told her admiringly.

'That,' said Caitlin, 'is because you're a guy. Guys don't think. Period.'

❧ CHAPTER 8 ❧

'The visions of romance were over.'
(Jane Austen, *Northanger Abbey*)

CAITLIN WOKE TO THE SOUND OF A BANGING DOOR. SHE
peered, bleary-eyed, at her bedside clock. Ten minutes
past midnight. If that was Summer, she'd have the
whole house awake.

'Good God, no!'

Caitlin's heart sank. Sir Magnus! He must have
discovered that Summer was missing, or worse still,
bumped into her as she crept back into the house.

She threw back the sheet and grabbed her bathrobe.
Padding to the door she peered out. It seemed all hell
had been let loose.

'Bloody fool!' Sir Magnus was shouting downstairs.
'What possessed you to let him go, Gaby?'

'I'm not responsible for every member of your family,
you know, whatever you may like to think! I'll get the
car.'

'Someone ought to tell Summer and Caitlin,' she
heard Ludo protest. At the mention of Summer's name,

Caitlin hurtled downstairs. The family were gathered in the entrance hall, and Caitlin's stomach did a double somersault, although more at the sight of Ludo in his boxer shorts than anything else.

'What's going on?' Caitlin asked. 'What's happened?'

'Now just sit down and stay calm,' Gabriella ordered her, pulling a sweatshirt over her pyjama top. 'They say it's not nearly as bad as it might have been . . .'

'That idiot brother of mine took Izzy out on the bike,' Ludo told her. 'They've had an accident.'

'Oh my God . . .'

Caitlin could see the headlines already: *Politician's daughter unconscious after spree with millionaire's son . . . Boyfriend mad with grief . . . Family gather at bedside . . . 'I warned her,' says teenage friend.*

'According to the police, they were swerving all over the place and the bike's wing mirror clipped a car coming the other way,' Gaby explained. 'Then they came off the road and crashed into a ditch. Lucky for them, they were being followed by a police car. It had just overtaken them and was flashing them to slow down – otherwise, God knows what might have happened.'

'Are they OK?'

'They're having X-rays now,' Ludo said. 'We must get going. Caitlin, you'll stay with Summer, right? Don't wake her, though – no point worrying her till we know more. Oh – and your brother, you'd better tell him.'

'I'll go and wake him – he'll want to go with you,' Caitlin said. 'After all, Izzy is his girlfriend.'

Not so you'd notice, she thought. I never did like that Freddie.

For the next hour and a half, Caitlin lay in bed trying, without success, to fall asleep. After everyone had left, she had made a hot drink to try to stop herself shaking. Jamie had been as white as a sheet at the news, and she'd so wanted to go along to the hospital for moral support – but, of course, she had to pretend to be on hand for when Summer woke up. She wished she would hurry up and come home; the house was so quiet and with no one to talk to she kept imagining the worst.

Finally, tired of tossing and turning, she got up and went along to Summer's room just in case she'd crept home so quietly that Caitlin hadn't heard her come in. The room was empty. She opened the cupboard and took out the paintings. This was her chance.

She nipped back to her room, got her camera and flashed off half a dozen shots of the pictures, before homing in and taking close-ups of different elements of each scene. It wouldn't be as good as having the pictures themselves, but if she mounted the photos together with the close-up of the painting of the boat, she could make something of them.

She wandered downstairs, peering out of windows as she went in the hope of seeing a car turning into the driveway. It was when she passed the den at the far end of the corridor that she spotted the laptop. And it was switched on.

It was obviously fate. The opportunity she'd been

looking for to find out about the abbey. It took a bit of fiddling but eventually she was on to Google. *Abbeys of Italy*, she typed. There were loads. *Abbeys of Liguria* – that would narrow it down a bit.

She scrolled through the results – San Anna, San Antimo . . . this was useless. They looked nothing like the picture on the sketch pad. Perhaps she was wasting her time; after all, apart from that one sketch, it wasn't as if Summer's mother had painted abbeys. The art of Elena Cumani-Tilney was far more exciting than that – all those grotesque images, storms and desecration; it was the sort of thing the tutors at her summer school the previous year had challenged her to think about when she was preparing for her GCSE . . .

What if The Abbey was the name of some kind of college or further education place where people could go and paint? Perhaps these painting holidays were courses in Art. Maybe that was it.

The Abbey she typed. The results flashed up on the screen. *The Abbey School*: no good – red brick and no turret; *The Abbey School of Catering* – hideous 1960s concrete monstrosity; *The Abbey Centre for Psychiatric Respite Care*. That one looked pretty much like it, but it was a hospital and . . .

'*Remember when she had to have time out, to get away . . . her best stuff was done when she was at the abbey . . . She took me in a boat at midnight . . . scared . . . slept in the rain and got soaked. Mum was quirky – all artists are . . . she did some silly things . . .*'

The words leaped into her mind of their own accord

as Caitlin scanned the screen a second time. Her mouth went dry and her heart began pounding.

The Abbey Centre for Psychiatric Respite Care. She double-clicked on the entry.

The Abbey Centre occupies a stunning position on the South Downs overlooking the seaside town of Eastbourne . . . patients are able to enjoy excellent recreational and therapeutic facilities . . . appropriate treatments to enable rehabilitation into the community and family life . . .

Caitlin stared and stared at the screen. Eastbourne was only twenty miles or so from Brighton. What's more, the photograph on the home page was identical to the drawing in the pad.

So that was where she went for her so-called painting holidays. And that was why—

'What are you doing?'

Caitlin screamed and twirled round in the chair. Ludo stood in the doorway, staring at her incredulously.

'You made me jump,' she gasped, leaping out of the chair and turning her back to the screen. 'I didn't hear a car. How are they? How's Izzy?'

'I said, what are you doing?' Ludo repeated.

'I couldn't sleep – I was just surfing the net for my art project. Summer said it would be OK.'

'Really.' He walked past her and stared at the screen. His shoulders sagged and he closed his eyes briefly.

'Doesn't look much like an art project to me,' he snapped, shaking his head in disbelief. 'So. The Abbey. So, Summer knows.'

He closed his eyes and gripped the back of the chair.

'No!' Caitlin stammered. 'I only just found it myself.'

'And how come you were looking in the first place? I know you were asking Gaby loads of stuff yesterday about abbeys. Who's been talking?'

'I – well, I can't really say because I'm not supposed to let on and . . .'

The sound of voices in the hall made Ludo turn and hold up a hand to silence her.

'Say nothing,' he muttered, grabbing the mouse and closing down the screen. 'We'll talk later.'

'I'm really sorry . . .' she began.

'So am I,' Ludo sighed, avoiding her gaze. 'You'll never know how sorry.'

'Poor you,' Gaby said, smiling, as Caitlin greeted her in the hall. 'Couldn't you sleep?'

'I was worried,' she gabbled. 'How are they?'

'Izzy's broken her ankle and her left wrist and she's got quite a few cuts and bruises,' Sir Magnus told her. 'Freddie's cracked a couple of ribs and dislocated his elbow. They were damn lucky – they could have been killed.'

'The hospital's keeping them in overnight and all being well they will be home tomorrow,' Gaby added. 'Jamie insisted on staying with Izzy – such a dear boy.'

'Pity the *dear boy* didn't stop her going with Freddie in the first place,' Sir Magnus muttered. 'Now I've got to telephone Isabella's father and tell him what my damn fool son has done.'

He ran a hand through his hair and yawned.

'Does Summer know what's happened?'

Caitlin shook her head. 'She's asleep – I thought it best, you know, with the migraine and all . . .'

'Quite right.' Sir Magnus nodded. 'Nice to know *someone* round here has some common sense.'

Caitlin lay staring at the ceiling. Ludo hadn't smiled at her, hadn't even glanced in her direction since finding her at the computer. He was furious, she could tell. He'd probably never speak to her again, much less fall in love with her—

'Magnus! Ludo! Come quickly!'

Gabriella's panic-stricken cries left Caitlin in no doubt as to what was the matter. Doors slammed and she could hear footsteps hurrying along the landing.

'It's Summer – she's not in her room!' she heard Gaby cry. 'Her bed hasn't been slept in.'

'*What?*'

'I don't believe it – get Caitlin!'

'She's probably asleep,' Gaby protested.

'Well, wake her,' Ludo ordered. 'If anyone knows what's going on, she will.'

'I'm sure she'll be back soon,' Caitlin faltered as she faced the grim faces of Sir Magnus, Gabriella and Ludo. 'She probably went for a walk to clear her head – you know, the migraine . . .'

'Clearly,' Gabriella snapped, 'you're not a migraine sufferer. She wouldn't have been able to lift her head from the pillow, never mind go walkabout.'

She ran her hand through her dishevelled hair.

'Have you searched the whole house?' Summer's father demanded. 'Perhaps she went to the bathroom and fainted . . .'

'What do you take me for?' Gabriella shouted, close to tears. 'I looked everywhere before I called you.'

'I'm going to call the police,' Sir Magnus declared, walking over to the desk. 'Please God, I'm not going through what I went through with her mother . . .'

He caught himself in time and started punching numbers into the phone. Caitlin's mind was in turmoil. Maybe she should tell them – what if Summer and Alex had decided to run away together tonight? What if Summer had lied to her and all that story about Milan was just a cover-up? Or worse, what if Alex was full of evil intentions after all? What if he'd asked her to meet him because he intended to kill her . . .

Teenager withholds vital information – friend found dead in olive grove.

'Stop!' she shouted. 'I know where she's gone. She didn't have a headache – she was going to meet someone.'

Sir Magnus let the phone fall from his hands as the clock chimed two.

'And I think,' she added, her voice wobbling, 'they might have run away.'

Summer's father sank into the chair and stared at her, his face draining of colour.

'They?' he murmured.

'Her and . . .' Caitlin felt as if she was betraying Summer with every syllable, but faced with the three of them, she had no choice. 'Her and Alex.'

'Alex? Alex di Matteo? Oh dear God, please no!'

'Alex – damn it! I knew it was him I saw that day . . .' Ludo gasped.

Gabriella simply closed her eyes and looked as if she was about to burst into tears.

'Caitlin, you have to tell us everything you know,' Ludo stressed. 'Everything.'

'I can't, I promised—'

'You are a guest in my house!' Sir Magnus stormed. 'If you've been colluding with my daughter over some hare-brained scheme . . .'

'Dad, stop it!' Ludo burst out. 'Are you really surprised that whatever Summer's done, it's going to be a friend she confides in? Because she sure as hell can't confide in us. Because we don't *do* truth, do we?'

'Ludo—'

'No, listen – what planet are you on? If Summer has run away – and God knows, it's possible – *we're* the ones to blame, not Caitlin. Did you honestly think, Dad, that you could get away with pulling the wool over her eyes forever?'

'Be quiet, Ludo,' Gabriella cut in, jerking her head in Caitlin's direction.

'Oh, don't worry,' Ludo snapped, his face now scarlet. 'She knows all about The Abbey. She's not stupid – and what's more important, neither is Summer. She's sixteen, for God's sake, not some blinkered kid.'

'It's over and done with,' Sir Magnus insisted. 'In the past. Forgotten.'

'Get real, Dad! Who was it that said it's the secrets we don't know that hurt us the most? Freddie may choose to drown it all out with drink and substances and God knows what else – oh, you didn't really think all that energy and buzz was natural, did you? – and of course, you've already decided that I had to be the good guy, and keep it all buttoned in – well, stuff that, Dad! I've had it up to here with secrets. I'm glad Caitlin found out about The Abbey.'

'Are you telling me that Summer knows about her mother's illness?' Sir Magnus gasped.

'Not yet,' Ludo retorted. 'But when – if – we find her, don't think you can bluster and boss and bully this time. She has a right to know. She *needs* to know.'

Gabriella nodded slowly.

'Ludo's got a point,' she admitted. 'But right now, finding Summer is the priority. Before it's too late.'

'And you've told us everything?' Sir Magnus demanded, after Caitlin had described the meeting in the church, the holdall and what she'd heard of the conversation between Alex and Summer.

'Yes,' she said, nodding. 'I couldn't hear everything they said but it was definitely about getting away and she asked Alex to take her with him.'

'But they haven't seen one another in two years,' Sir Magnus began.

'If it was Alex I saw in Brighton that evening when I was looking for Summer – well, then, they obviously *have* seen one another,' Ludo pointed out.

Caitlin was about to confirm his suspicions, but thought better of it. Right now, keeping quiet seemed the safest option.

At that moment, there was an urgent knocking at the back door.

'Summer!' Gabriella and Ludo cried in unison. Thank God for that, Caitlin thought, as Sir Magnus slid the bolt and opened the door.

It wasn't Summer who stepped over the threshold.

It was Alex.

And he was alone.

'Is Summer here?' Alex was panting and beads of perspiration stood out on his forehead. 'I didn't mean to upset her . . .'

'What have you done with her? Where is she?' Caitlin shouted. 'I should never have believed her – I knew all along you were up to no good and it's my fault . . .'

'Caitlin, stop.' Ludo laid a hand on her shoulder. 'Let Alex speak.'

'And make it quick,' Sir Magnus ordered. 'If you know where my daughter is and you don't tell me, so help me, I'll have the police on to you . . .'

'Dad! Let the guy speak!'

Alex swallowed hard and looked Summer's father in the eye.

'We arranged to meet tonight, right? I'm staying in Vernazza with my gran, and she's got it into her head that she wants to go to Milan at the weekend and . . .'

'Yes, yes, get on with it!' stormed Sir Magnus.

'Anyway, we were just chatting and then Summer

began talking about us getting engaged soon.'

'*Engaged?*' Caitlin thought Sir Magnus was about to have a heart attack on the spot. 'What a load of juvenile nonsense! You haven't seen one another in ages.'

'We've been seeing each other off and on all year,' Alex retorted. 'As often as she could *get away*,' he added pointedly.

'You've been what? Don't be so stupid – I've made damn sure she's been in Brighton with me and . . .'

'I've been in Brighton too – on a university exchange,' Alex said, his voice cracking with suppressed emotion. 'And please will you just let me finish before you say any more?'

Sir Magnus nodded abruptly, sinking on to one of the bar stools and resting his chin on his hands.

'We played together as kids, right?' Alex went on, glancing at Ludo who nodded in agreement. 'When we moved back to the States, I really missed her, so when I got to the UK, it was pretty obvious I was going to get in touch. I even said as much to my dad—'

'And he didn't have the decency to stop you?' Sir Magnus blurted out.

'Magnus, for God's sake, let the boy speak!' Gabriella shouted.

'Oh, sure he did – that was what set hares running in my head,' Alex explained. 'He virtually forbade me to get in touch with any of you. He said . . .'

He faltered.

'Go on,' Ludo encouraged him.

'He said that the Tilneys were the past and the past was best left alone.'

'That,' said Sir Magnus, 'is probably the most sensible remark to come out of your father's mouth in a long time.'

'I wish he'd told me the truth then,' Alex admitted. 'But he didn't. Not till I told him I was in love with Summer—'

'Love? What do you kids know of love?'

'Enough to know that when you love someone you can't keep secrets from them, and that's what I would have to do. That's why I hung back. I thought it best if we just took things dead slowly, till I had a chance to talk to you and . . . well, anyway, that's why tonight, when she talked about getting engaged, I kept trying to change the subject, saying we were too young, she was still at school, all that stuff.'

'So you weren't going to elope?' Caitlin burst out.

'Elope? Are you mad?' Alex eyed her with disdain.

'What happened next?' Sir Magnus's voice was shaky as he took a step towards Alex.

'Sum got really tearful and in the end I said it was getting late and she ought to be getting home, and then she went ballistic. She suddenly got it into her head that I wasn't going to Milan with Gran at all, but going off with some other girl.'

He paused, eyeing everyone anxiously.

'That's when I flipped,' he admitted. 'I told her that we had no future if she was going to go on and on all the time about her mum. I said that she was dead and we were alive and . . . and then I told her.'

'Told her what? That it was over?' There was a note of hope in Sir Magnus's voice.

'No. I told her about my dad and her mum.'

Oh my God, thought Caitlin. They had an affair.

'After that, she burst into tears and ran off. I chased after her, but I couldn't find her. I came here, because I had to know she was OK.'

'Well thanks to you she's not,' Sir Magnus stormed. 'What *were* you thinking of?'

'Don't you get it?' By now Alex was shouting. 'I felt so guilty – I wanted to come clean with her about all the other stuff. But she ran off before—'

'What other stuff?' Ludo asked, his jaw working with emotion and his eyes narrowed in what seemed to Caitlin like fear.

'*Allo moto, allo moto . . .*'

'What on earth is that?' Gaby asked.

'It's my mobile,' Caitlin gasped. 'I must have left it in my camera bag.'

She ran over to the coat hooks by the back door and unzipped her bag, grabbing the phone and flipping open the lid.

'Summer?' Everyone turned to stare at her, relief flooding their faces. 'Thank God – where are you?'

She swallowed hard, trying to keep her face expressionless as Summer sobbed and babbled down the phone.

'Yeah, OK – I'll come. Where are you? Yes, I know. Give me ten minutes. OK, bye.'

She stuffed the phone back into her bag.

'What the hell do you think you're doing?' Sir Magnus demanded. 'What's all this "give me ten minutes" nonsense? You should have told her to get back here and—'

'Oh, and you really think that if I'd said you were all waiting to pounce on her, she'd have come running back?' Caitlin retorted, not caring if she sounded rude. 'If you must know, she's not far – she saw the lights on in the house and knew she couldn't get back unnoticed. She's in a right state; she's my friend, and, if you don't mind, *she's* the one that matters right now.'

Caitlin put her arm round Summer as they squatted on the ground in a grove of olive trees overlooking Casa Vernazza.

'He's got someone else, I know he has,' Summer sobbed. 'He was really horrid about my mum, making out that she'd . . . well, done things I know she'd never, ever have done.'

She wiped her nose on the back of her hand.

'Then he said . . . oh God, what am I going to do without him? I love him so much – except that right now I hate him, but I thought . . .'

'Come on,' Caitlin demanded, standing up and pulling Summer to her feet. 'We're going home.'

'Oh, like that's a good plan,' Summer snapped. 'The lights are still on – why's everyone up?'

'Well, you're not to worry, but Freddie and Izzy had a bit of a prang on the bike,' Caitlin said. 'They're OK –

but everyone's been to the hospital and um – they found out you weren't in bed.'

'Oh no!'

'It's OK,' Caitlin lied. 'I said you'd probably gone for a stroll to clear your head.'

That much is true, she thought. It's just the rest of it that's going to be tricky to explain away.

'Before we go in,' Caitlin began tentatively as she and Summer reached the back door, 'there's something I should mention . . .'

The door was flung open and Sir Magnus opened his arms.

'Thank God!' He enveloped his daughter in a hug, and Caitlin was sure there were tears in his eyes. 'Don't you ever, ever put us through anything like that again as long as you live.'

He grasped her hand and led her into the kitchen. Caitlin followed, holding her breath.

'Alex!'

Summer dropped her father's hand, her eyes flitting round the four people in the room. She wheeled round and turned on Caitlin.

'You told them! They went after him . . . You despicable, beastly, hateful—'

'Hang on!' Alex shouted at her. 'I came here of my own free will.'

'You did *what*? How come?'

'Because, you silly, I was worried sick about you.'

'Oh sure, so worried that you're going off with some

{172}

other girl; so worried that you had to lie about my mum . . .'

She checked herself and looked anxiously at her father.

'Listen, Summer, I love you but—' Alex began.

'Enough!' Sir Magnus held up a hand. 'It's nearly three and we are all shattered. We will sort this mess out in the morning. Alex, your grandmother will be worried . . .'

'No, she won't,' he admitted. 'I said I'd be out all night . . . well, I mean . . . that is, I'd be back late and . . .'

'Right,' Sir Magnus ordered. 'Alex, you can sleep in the Garden House – Jamie's bed's free because he's with Izzy. Oh no – I forgot. I'll have to phone her parents . . .'

'In the morning,' Gaby said firmly. 'It's not as if Izzy is at death's door.'

'You're right, as usual.' Sir Magnus gave Gaby a kiss on her forehead and turned to the others.

'Nine o'clock tomorrow we sort this out – once and for all. Sleep well. And Summer . . .'

'Yeah?'

'I love you.'

A persistent tapping on her bedroom door woke Caitlin from a fitful sleep.

'Who is it?'

'Ludo.'

She leaped out of bed and then straight back in again as she realised she was stark naked. Scrabbling under her pillow for her PJs, she ran a hand through her hair, squirted some Eau d'Amour all over her and ran to the door.

'Hi.' It was, she thought regretfully, extremely hard to look and sound sexy after four hours' sleep and two nightmares.

'I know it's early but I'm going for a swim. Will you come? Please? We need to talk.'

Caitlin didn't have to be asked twice.

'Who told you about The Abbey?' Ludo asked as they swam towards the deep end of the pool, away from the house. 'You can't just have found it by chance.'

'Yes, I did I just—'

'Caitlin, please. Don't do this to me.' Ludo flipped over on to his back and stood up. 'I need to know the truth – it's important.'

'Someone said that your mum's best work was done at The Abbey and I thought – *we* thought – it was maybe an old ruin,' Caitlin admitted, because she couldn't bear to upset him further. 'But then we got hold of this sketch that she'd done and when I looked on the internet, I found a photo that was identical.'

'Where did you find the sketch?' Ludo didn't look at her but merely splashed the water idly with his hand.

'It was given to Summer,' she replied hesitantly.

'Go on,' Ludo ordered.

Caitlin decided that, since any hope she'd ever entertained of being in the bosom of the Tilney family was over, and since Ludo couldn't give a toss about her, she might as well spill the beans and get it over with. She told him about Lorenzo, the gallery in Vernazza, the picture of the boat . . .

'My God, she did a picture of that?' Ludo turned to Caitlin, a look of genuine astonishment on his face. 'She nearly killed herself and Summer that night.'

'What?'

'Oh, not deliberately – but she was in one of her manic phases.'

He paused.

'My mum was bipolar,' he whispered.

'What's that?'

'She was a manic depressive,' he muttered. 'She was beautiful, talented, could be really lovely – and sometimes she'd be fine for months on end. But it never lasted.'

He sighed. 'She was mentally ill, Caitlin. She had delusions, she heard voices. And in the end, it killed her.'

'But Summer never said . . .'

'That's the whole point,' Ludo stressed. 'Summer never had it explained to her. I guess at some level she must have known, certainly as she got older; but she just seemed to blank out all the bad bits. She always seems to concentrate on the good times; she just forgets all those weeks when Mum was at The Abbey; she overlooks the holidays out here when by the end of a month we were actually desperate to go home to the UK so Mum could get more treatment; she forgets how Freddie and I were told to keep her amused, never to say what was wrong with our mother . . .'

'So *you* knew?'

'Not at first – but, don't forget, we're nearly four years

older than Summer. By the time we were old enough to start being embarrassed by her odd behaviour, Dad simply said she was ill in her mind and that we must be nice to her and above all, not talk about it to anyone. Ever.'

'Why? I mean, it wasn't *her* fault . . .'

'This family don't talk to one another about deep stuff at the best of times,' Ludo replied, splashing water on his face. 'Dad's the stiff-upper-lip type – image is all. Not washing the dirty linen in public and all that stuff.'

He sighed wearily.

'They stopped entertaining much – except for Alex's family and Gaby, of course and no one came round to our place. It's my guess that Dad was scared Mum would say . . .'

He rubbed his eyes wearily.

'Say what?'

'Oh – nothing. Just something Dad doesn't think Freddie or I know about. It's not important. And to be fair, Dad did his best. See, Mum would ignore us for weeks on end, and I mean *ignore* – no meals ready, no outings. That's why we went off to boarding school when we were so young – Dad wanted us to have a semblance of normal life.'

Caitlin frowned.

'I still don't get it,' she admitted. 'I mean, why didn't Summer go to boarding school too?'

'Because Summer was the one person that kept Mum together. If Summer was around, she'd hold it together. Just.'

Caitlin detected the faintest note of jealousy in his voice.

'Oh sure,' he went on hastily, 'she still had her moments, like the boat trip . . .'

'And sleeping out in the rain?'

'You heard about that? Summer sure opens up to you.' There was a note of admiration in Ludo's voice now.

'I think I get it!' Caitlin gasped. 'That's why Summer thinks it's all her fault her mum died. That's why she blames herself.'

'She does *what*?'

'She says if she hadn't gone on that trip to America, your mum would still be alive. You know, she could have protected her from your father's rages, kept her safe, stopped him having the affair with Gaby . . .'

'Bloody hell! Is that what she really thinks?'

Ludo's hand slammed the water.

'That does it,' he burst out. 'I'm calling time. This farce has gone on long enough.'

He climbed out of the pool and pushed the foot pedal of the shower.

'Get dried,' he ordered. 'And wake Summer up. I've had it up to here with my family.'

Despite the obvious urgency of the situation, Caitlin couldn't resist throwing one last glance at Ludo's wet chest and tight bum. He looked so masterful when he was angry.

And he was so principled. She liked that in a guy.

Sir Magnus had insisted that everyone gathered round the breakfast table, but no one felt hungry enough to eat.

{177}

Summer, pale and red-eyed, slumped at one end, ignoring Alex's weak smiles; Gabriella stifled yawns and sipped at a glass of orange juice while Ludo drummed the table with his fingers, his energy like that of a volcano about to erupt.

'I've spoken to Isabella's father,' Sir Magnus said, pouring himself some coffee. 'He wants her flown home to see some bone specialist. He's phoning our hospital today to get more information.'

'But Jamie . . .' Caitlin began.

'From what he said, Jamie is not his favourite person right now,' Sir Magnus commented. 'However, enough of that. We have more important things to discuss.'

He turned to Alex.

'Am I right in thinking that your father told you about – well, told you what Elena felt about . . .'

'Yes.'

Alex didn't meet his gaze but seemed to be inspecting the quarry tiles on the floor in minute detail.

'It all fell into place when he explained,' he muttered. 'Stuff I'd seen, things I'd overheard . . . but it wasn't his fault that she . . .'

'Of course it wasn't,' Gabriella broke in at once. 'In fact, if anyone was to blame it was me.'

It was as if someone had sent an electrical charge through Summer's body.

'*You!* I knew it was you – you hated her, you made her life . . .'

She flew across the kitchen and punched Gaby in the shoulder.

'I hate you, I hate . . .'

Millionaire's mistress in double intrigue – 'I was there,'
says teenager.

Caitlin knew that *Prego* magazine would pay mega-
bucks for this kind of story. She also knew that she would
never be able to write it. Which was a pity.

'Summer, no! No!' Sir Magnus pulled Summer away
but instead of shouting at her as Caitlin had expected,
he enveloped her in a hug and wouldn't let her go.

'Leave me alone, leave me alone!' Summer struggled
and wriggled but Sir Magnus refused to release her.

'Your mum and I were friends for years, you know
that,' Gaby said, fighting back tears. 'I always said to her
that when she was having a bad patch I'd be there for
her. Only that day, I wasn't.'

Summer said nothing, but her sobs abated a little.

'She came to my cottage – I know that because she
left a note. The note simply said, *Where are you? It's bad
bad bad. Help me now.*'

Gaby pressed her lips together, took a deep breath and
went on.

'I was staying with friends in Rapallo; your dad had had
to fly back to London for an emergency board meeting.
She would have wanted someone around. She knew
where I hid the key and she must have let herself in.'

'And?' Summer's voice was muffled as her father still
held her close to him.

'We're not sure,' Gaby sighed. 'But she'd clearly drunk
a lot of stuff – the gin was half drunk, two empty wine
bottles were flung on the floor and the police found a
vodka bottle in the bushes outside.'

She glanced at Magnus and he nodded imperceptibly.

'As the police pointed out, all that alcohol would have played havoc with her medication . . .'

'Medication? What medication?'

Summer pulled away from her father and stared dully at Gaby.

'She took pills to help her cope – you must remember that,' Gaby said.

'Oh – her indigestion pills.' Summer shrugged. 'She said she only needed them when I wasn't there because my cooking was so nice.'

Caitlin wondered how much longer her friend could go on deceiving herself. But when she caught her eye, she realised from Summer's anguished expression that the words didn't match the thoughts that were battling in her mind.

'So who called the police?' Summer demanded.

'Alex's father,' said Sir Magnus. 'He found the body when he was walking his dog and he told them where she was. They questioned him hard of course, and that's when it all came out. He told them.'

'Told them what, Dad?' Summer's tone was firmer now. 'I want to know it all.'

'Summer, not now – not here. It's private, it's not for everyone to—'

'Dad. Caitlin's my best mate, Alex is – was – my boyfriend . . . and you're my family. Spit it out, for God's sake. I'm sick of not knowing the truth. Except that—'

She hesitated.

'Except that, I think I do know it now. I think I've known it deep down for a very long time.'

She wrung her hands together and swallowed back tears.

'She was mad, wasn't she? That's what Mr di Matteo told the police. That my mother was mad.'

'She wasn't mad!' Gabriella shouted. 'Your mum was a sweet, talented, funny, lovely person, who happened to have bouts of mental illness that made it hard for her to distinguish between reality and delusion. But she wasn't mad. Just ill.'

Summer lifted her face from her father's chest and eyed Gabriella with something approaching gratitude.

Just then, the phone on the wall began shrilling and Gaby moved to answer it.

'Leave it,' Ludo begged her. 'Please – let's get this over and done with. At least now I don't have to keep secrets any more.'

'You? You knew all about this stuff?' Summer gasped.

'I knew about Mum's illness, sure.' Ludo shrugged. 'Just like you did. You did, didn't you?'

Summer swallowed.

'I knew she was – different,' she said, nodding. 'But I knew I could keep her safe. She told me that all the time, from when I was very little. "God sent you to me to keep me safe. Without you I'd . . ."'

Summer choked.

'"Without you, I'd go mad," that's what she'd say.'

Her voice caught in a sob.

'And I wasn't there, and she *did* go mad.'

'No, darling . . .' Gaby began.

Summer took a deep breath, and then, tears streaming down her face, she walked resolutely out of the room.

Caitlin was sitting by the pool, idly splashing her feet in the water, when Ludo appeared.

'Sorry about all that,' he murmured. 'You must wish you'd never come.'

'Of course I don't,' Caitlin assured him. 'I'm just glad it's all getting sorted.'

'*Sorted?*' Ludo sneered. 'For *her* maybe. For me – fat chance!'

And with that, he dived into the pool and began slicing through the water as if his life depended on it.

Caitlin was sketching half-heartedly at the edge of the terrace when she saw Summer and Alex coming towards her, hand in hand.

'So you two are OK now?' she said delightedly. 'I'm so pleased . . .'

'What's going on?' Ludo, still dripping wet from his frenetic swimming, literally ran across the terrace towards them. 'What's with the hand holding?'

'Chill, Ludo,' Summer said. 'Alex has explained everything and we're fine now and—'

'No bloody way!' Ludo shouted, and the venom in his voice made Caitlin physically flinch. 'Do you mean Dad's still not coming clean?'

'What do you mean? Clean about what?' Alex gasped.

'Come with me,' Ludo ordered. 'I've had enough of

keeping my mouth shut. I can't bear it any longer. My sister's been through enough. You too, Caitlin – you need to hear the truth as well.'

For heaven's sake, Ludo, what's all this about?' Sir Magnus, red-eyed with exhaustion, lowered himself heavily into a leather armchair in his study where they'd found him filing papers.

'It's about all these secrets,' Ludo stormed. 'You can't do this, Dad. Summer really does love Alex.'

'I know, son.' Sir Magnus nodded. 'And I agree, they're young and it'll probably all blow over, but until it does—'

'Which it won't,' Summer cut in.

'. . . there's no harm in it, I suppose. At least, that's how Gaby sees it.'

'*No harm?* Are you stark staring, raving mad? You told me that I was to make sure that the two of them never got together again, right?'

'Yes, but that was because I hoped Summer wouldn't need to find out about Elena's illness – she had her on such a pedestal and I didn't want her memory sullied for her.'

'Oh right!' Ludo shouted. 'Well, I know that's only half the reason. Go on, tell her the rest. Tell her now.'

'Ludo, I don't know what you're talking about,' Sir Magnus shouted.

'Tell her that Alex is her half-brother,' Ludo said.

The colour drained from Summer's face and she began to sway. In an instant, Ludo was at her side, his arms supporting her as he led her gently to a chair. Despite

{183}

the drama of the situation, Caitlin couldn't help a flash of envy and the thought that perhaps, one day, a touch of sunstroke while walking with Ludo might be an awfully good idea.

'Get her some water someone,' Sir Magnus cried, rushing to her side and sinking to his knees. 'And Summer, listen. It's not true. You are *my* child. I swear it on – on my life.'

He took his daughter's hand and looked at her pleadingly.

'Dad, Freddie overheard you and Alex's dad arguing about it years ago,' Ludo protested. 'You can't pretend . . .'

'Sure we argued,' Sir Magnus said. 'We argued terrifically. I told him I never wanted to see him again.'

'Yeah, because he was—'

'Enough!' Sir Magnus took Summer's hand, and gestured to Ludo and Alex to follow him out of the room.

Caitlin made to follow them, agog to hear the latest in this bizarre family history. But before she could reach the door, Sir Magnus had slammed it firmly in her face.

She had thought of wandering down the hallway to eavesdrop, but despite almost dying of curiosity she couldn't bring herself to be that deceitful. She sat in the garden room, idly flicking through Italian magazines that she couldn't understand and listening to the monotonous ticking of the carriage clock on the sideboard.

Eventually, she heard footsteps and Summer

appeared, her cheeks streaked with mascara, but looking decidedly more cheerful.

'What happened?' Caitlin gasped. 'I mean, you don't have to tell me, but . . .'

'But you'll burst if I don't!' The ghost of a smile hovered on Summer's lips. 'I'm going to say this once and then please, let's forget it, OK?'

Caitlin nodded.

'Apparently, a year or so before she died, Mum started telling people that I was . . . well, that I was a love child,' Summer whispered. 'She said that Alex's dad was my father.'

'But it wasn't true?'

'No, it was all part of her delusions.'

She swallowed hard.

'Apparently, she fell in love with Alex's dad and convinced herself that he was in love with her too. She used to go round to their house – she'd throw herself at Alex's dad and kiss him and cry and say that she couldn't bear to be parted from him. It took Mr di Matteo a long time to convince Alex's mum that he was innocent. That's why she never liked it when Mum went round to their house.'

'I can see why,' Caitlin gasped.

'She told this story about me being conceived on the beach after a late-night party and what was so convincing, Dad says, is that there *was* a party about nine months before I was born – Alex's dad's birthday or something.'

Love child or legitimate heiress? Our inside reporter, Caitlin Morland, ferrets out the truth.

The headlines formed themselves in Caitlin's imagination.

'But he didn't believe the story?'

Summer chewed on a fingernail.

'No, because he'd been at that party and he and Mum had been together all the time. Besides, the doctors had told him over and over again about Mum becoming more delusional. But . . .'

'But what?'

'At the funeral, Alex's dad kept asking how I was doing, whether I'd like to spend some time in America with his family . . . and Dad got suspicious and wondered if he'd been kidding himself after all.'

'And?'

'He decided to get a DNA test done just to make sure,' Summer went on. 'So when I was asleep he cut off a bit of my hair and sent it off to one of those labs you see advertised on the internet.'

'It's like that programme – what's it called? *Silent Witness*,' Caitlin interrupted.

'And it's OK, I'm his,' Summer said. 'Thank goodness.'

It occurred to Caitlin that for someone who was supposed to hate her father, Summer looked intensely relieved.

'And what about Alex? Where is he?'

'He's getting ready to take take his gran to Milan,' Summer replied. 'Then we're going for a walk. But guess what? Dad's invited him to stay when he gets back.'

'Ace!' Caitlin grinned. 'So he approves?'

'Let's put it this way,' Summer said. 'He said he wants

to get to know him better, which for my father is almost the equivalent of a partnership in the family firm.'

'You must be over the moon.'

'To be honest, my head's still spinning over all this stuff with Mum. I just hope they won't all go back to avoiding any mention of her name.'

'They won't,' Caitlin said confidently.

'How do you know?'

'Trust me,' smiled Caitlin. 'I'm good like that.'

'Hey, Ludo!' Caitlin ran across the terrace to where Ludo was leaning on the balustrade, staring pensively into the middle distance. 'So it's all cleared up? You must be so relieved.'

Ludo sighed.

'Yes, I guess,' he said. 'At least I now know why Dad told me and Freddie to make sure Alex and Summer never got in touch.'

'Well, that's the bit I don't get,' Caitlin admitted. 'I mean, since he knows that all that business about her being a love child is rubbish, why would it matter?'

'Because Dad, for all his faults, knew that Summer had put her mum on a pedestal. He thought that if it all came out – and let's face it, it's pretty embarrassing – Summer's memory of her might somehow be tainted.'

He glanced across the terrace.

'Quiet – she's coming over.' He waved at his sister. 'Hey, come and join us.'

There were a dozen questions buzzing through Caitlin's

brain all day but she had no chance to voice any of them. Jamie, Izzy and Freddie had arrived home early that afternoon; Jamie, exhausted by a night at Izzy's bedside, fell asleep on a sun lounger by the pool, and Freddie was closeted with his father behind closed doors, from where the sound of raised voices rang across the garden. Summer and Alex disappeared for a long walk and Caitlin was left with Izzy.

'I've really messed up, haven't I?' Izzy sighed, sipping an iced lemonade that Gabriella had brought to the poolside. 'Why can't I be sensible like you?'

'It wasn't your fault Freddie crashed the bike,' Caitlin reasoned. 'But you have been treating Jamie pretty horribly and if you don't mind me saying so, he deserves better.'

'I know,' Izzy admitted. 'I've been so dumb; I mean, if I hadn't come on to Freddie like I did, we wouldn't have been on the stupid bike in the first place.'

She glanced at Caitlin out of the corner of her eye.

'See, we were planning to go off round Italy together.'

'You were *what?*' Caitlin gasped. 'But you and Jamie were going to Venice . . .'

'I know, it was me who brought up the idea,' Izzy admitted. 'The plan was that Freddie would turn up after a couple of days, and I'd dump Jamie and go with him.'

Izzy avoided Caitlin's disbelieving gaze.

'You would have dumped my brother just like that?' Caitlin gasped. 'Are you mad? Can't you see Freddie for what he is – always high on something? He was probably drunk last night.'

Izzy nodded.

'He got breathalysed,' she admitted. 'And you're right – I've been so horrid to Jamie, ramming Freddie down his throat. And yet all the time I was in hospital, he was there. Just holding my hand and stopping me being scared.'

She turned to Caitlin.

'Freddie did nothing all the way home in the cab but talk about which bits of him were hurting,' she said. 'Like I hadn't even got a graze.'

Caitlin was too angry to meet her eye.

'And I suppose now, you want to crawl back to Jamie and pick up where you left off?' she demanded. 'Never mind that he's been hurt like hell and . . .'

'OK, there's no need to go on about it, I've got the message,' she said. 'I want to be friends with Jamie – but just friends. I don't reckon I'm ready to commit to anyone. Unlike you . . . So, how's it going with you and Ludo? Have you got it together yet?'

'No,' Caitlin said shortly.

'No?' repeated Izzy. 'What have you been doing all this time?'

⁊ CHAPTER 9 ⁊

'She was assured of his affection.'
(Jane Austen, *Northanger Abbey*)

'WHAT ARE YOU DOING?' CAITLIN WALKED UP BEHIND Ludo as he was sitting in a deck chair on the terrace, an open book in his hands.

'Nothing much, why?'

'I want you to do me a huge favour,' she said. She figured she had nothing to lose; he wasn't remotely interested in her romantically – but he did love his sister. 'Come to Vernazza with me. Get the picture that Summer loves so much.'

'I can't,' he replied flatly. 'Dad would go ballistic . . .'

'Ludo, you keep saying that your father shouldn't have kept secrets, that you're fed up with lies – but what are *you* doing about it? Zilch. Nothing.'

Ludo frowned but stayed silent.

'Your mum had a talent, right?'

'I guess,' he said.

'And your dad, for whatever reason, wanted it hidden away – I guess because he thought people would

{190}

ask questions and find out that all her best stuff was done when she was manic, right?'

'He knew if there was an exhibition, she'd get interviewed by the press and – well, you never knew with Mum quite what would come out. And I suppose all this business with Tony di Matteo was fresh in his mind. Imagine if she'd told the newspapers that Summer was . . .'

'OK,' Caitlin said. 'But your mother's dead and Summer's alive and she needs to have something positive about her mum to hang on to.'

Ludo looked at her long and hard.

'That's really perceptive.' He nodded slowly. 'I get where you're coming from.'

Page eleven of last month's *Secrets of the Stars* magazine, she thought. But hey – what's the point of reading if you can't toss out the odd quote now and then?

'OK,' Ludo conceded. 'I'll come with you. Actually, I fancy a walk – can you cope with four miles?'

'Of course I can.' She smiled. With you, I could cope with a marathon.

'Was she really talented?' Ludo asked after he'd spent fifteen minutes talking to Lorenzo and looking at the boat picture over and over again. 'I mean, would this picture actually sell for money?'

Lorenzo laughed. 'Only about eight hundred euros, maybe,' he told him. 'But this painting, it is a small one, and she paint it early in her career. Later, she became very good, very, how you say, *passionate* artist. These paintings – well, now we are talking several thousand euros.'

Ludo whistled through his teeth.

'OK – well, I'll take this one back for my sister,' he said resolutely. 'Thank you, Lorenzo. And if you find any others . . .'

'You will be first to know,' Lorenzo assured him. 'But you ask your father, eh? He have maybe fifty, hidden some place. Such waste – it is almost criminal.'

'Let's stop.'

Ludo sank down on to the grass at the side of the path, laid the picture carefully to one side and pulled Caitlin down beside him.

'It's not been much of a holiday for you so far, has it?' he said ruefully. 'You must be itching to go home, away from all the dramas.'

'No way,' Caitlin assured him. 'How could anyone want to leave all this?' She waved her hand at the view below them, at the azure-blue sea, the pastel painted houses and the yachts bobbing like toys in a toddler's bath.

'Will you paint it?' Ludo asked.

'I'd love to,' Caitlin said, nodding. 'But it seems a bit tactless in view of . . .'

'No, you must,' Ludo insisted. 'You said you had a school project?'

'Yes, but I've got an ace idea for that,' she told him eagerly. 'Only I'd need your help.'

'I'll do what I can,' he said.

'See, what I thought was . . .' She began. And stopped as his fingers delicately touched her lips.

'Before you say anything, I need to know something,' he said.

'What?'

'Is there anyone back at home?'

Caitlin frowned.

'Loads of them,' she said, puzzled. 'One brother, three sisters . . .'

'No, you muppet,' he said, laughing. 'I mean – a guy.'

She shook her head, not trusting herself to speak, and holding her breath.

'Oh good,' he said. 'Because ever since you threw that drink over me, I've been wanting to kiss you. And now seems as good a time as any.'

They were all wrong, Caitlin decided. Every magazine she had ever read, every description of falling in love, was way short of the mark. The six days, three hours and twenty-seven minutes since she had become Ludo's girlfriend (she liked to say the phrase over and over in her head) had been the happiest of her entire sixteen years and ten months. She felt prettier, cleverer, more confident than ever before; her painting – because Ludo had insisted that she paint – was flowing with an ease she'd never experienced; and nothing – not even the fact that Jamie had insisted on returning to the UK with Izzy despite being told that he was just a mate – *nothing* could lower her spirits.

'I guess you've had loads of girlfriends,' she had said to Ludo that first day.

'Hardly,' he had replied. 'Oh sure, there were girls I hung out with in the Sixth Form but it never worked out because I could never be myself with them. Asking them home was pretty much a non-starter, answering questions about family – well, you can guess what that was like. And besides . . .'

He had paused and cupped her face in his hands.

'You know what? You knowing *everything* and still being here, still fighting Summer's corner, still mucking in with all the mess that's my family – well, that makes it all possible somehow.'

He had broken off then, laughing and accusing her of turning him into 'a right wuss' – but it had been enough.

Caitlin had known that it was OK to ask him this one last favour.

It had taken a whole day to persuade Summer's father and another four days for him to get it organised, but now they were ready. Thankfully, Summer had been so occupied with Alex, who was due to leave the following day for America, that she hadn't taken much notice of Ludo and Caitlin, apart from hugging Caitlin on several occasions and saying how cool it was that they were an item and how when she and Alex got married (which of course wouldn't be for ages, but would definitely happen) Caitlin had to be chief bridesmaid.

Caitlin was the one detailed to lure Alex and Summer to the Garden House that evening.

'It won't take a minute,' she said, when Summer protested that they were about to go down to

Francesco's for a drink. 'You'll love it. Trust me.'

She led them across the courtyard and flung open the door.

'Oh!' Summer stood on the threshold, transfixed. Every inch of the whitewashed walls was covered with Elena's paintings. Some were tiny, pastel and pretty; others were huge, with great sweeps of vermilion, magenta, black and gold; there were landscapes, abstracts and two strange skyscapes showing stars with faces and a moon that was exploding into a hundred sparkling fragments.

But it was the picture on the far wall that Summer was staring at.

'It's us,' she breathed. 'It's her and me.'

The picture was unlike any other. Summer's mother had painted herself with a serene smile on her face, as she looked into the eyes of her daughter. Summer was shown laughing, her blond hair falling over one side of her face as she leaned towards her mother.

It was, Caitlin thought, as natural and as real as any photograph.

'It's beautiful,' Alex breathed. 'They're all amazing – but that one is stunning.'

Summer turned to her father, who had been standing quietly in the background.

'You got them back.' She stretched out a hand and he squeezed it. 'What made you do it?'

'Caitlin,' he said simply. 'She made me see that by hiding Elena's pictures away, I wasn't protecting her reputation, or stopping people from realising she was bipolar. All I was doing was preventing the world from enjoying her talent. Celebrating her gifts.'

He turned to Summer.

'I'm so sorry, darling,' he murmured. 'For everything. For not telling you the truth, for letting you think it was your fault . . .'

'Shall we give him the stuff?' Alex interrupted. 'Now seems like a good time.'

Summer smiled and nodded.

'It's in the old stable,' she said. 'I'll fetch it.'

Caitlin held her breath as Summer returned, clutching the holdall she'd seen in the church.

'Alex brought these back from Boston,' she told her father, pulling out several sheets of newspaper. 'Look.'

Caitlin edged closer to Sir Magnus in the hopes of reading over his shoulder.

'*Unknown artist's work surprise shock at auction,*' he read. '*Local restaurateur promises more to come.*'

'My dad had ten pictures of Elena's,' Alex explained. 'She insisted on giving them to him, and because of my mum's feelings he sold six of them – and they made a mint. He says he's going to auction the rest next year.'

'So that's what was in the bag! And all the time I thought you were going to run away,' Caitlin burst out.

'So you *did* see us,' Summer observed.

'Sorry,' Caitlin whispered. 'I didn't let on, though.'

'It's OK,' Summer said, with a laugh. 'I'm so happy now that I don't care.'

She turned to her father.

'See – when Alex showed me this cutting, I assumed that you'd sent the pictures overseas to be sold and not told me and . . .'

'As if I'd do that!' Sir Magnus cried. 'I only stored them away because they reminded me too much of her illness and my ineptitude in dealing with things. I grew to hate the smell of oil paint because it always heralded a bad patch.'

He touched Summer's shoulder.

'Would you like me to get the pictures back from Alex's dad?' he asked.

Summer shook her head.

'No,' she said. 'It's OK – but what's going to happen to all these?' She waved a hand at the paintings around her.

'How about you choose the ones you want to keep,' he said, 'and we set up a permanent exhibition in the village for the others? Give your mum the fame she deserves?'

So much for me being the one to introduce the world to the art of Elena Cumani-Tilney, thought Caitlin. She seems to have done it perfectly well herself . . . even from beyond the grave.

'I'm taking *Gina* out,' Ludo told Caitlin later that afternoon. 'Want to come?'

'Yes, please,' Caitlin replied eagerly. 'Don't know where Summer and Alex have got to, though.'

'Good, because they're not invited,' he said. 'This is just you and me. And before we go, we need to do some serious talking.'

Caitlin held her breath.

'For one thing, gossip magazines. Now, is it to be *Art uncovered – the exposé of hidden sins* for *Prego* magazine, or maybe, on second thoughts, would you do better with *Love, lies and lust in Liguria* for *Goss*?'

'I wouldn't – how could you think that?' Caitlin burst out, feeling somewhat guilty at just how accurately he had interpreted her daydreaming.

'I'm teasing you, silly,' he laughed, pulling her towards him. 'It's just that on the plane you were so keen on all those rubbishy magazines and so adamant that you read serious stuff too . . .'

'I do!'

'I guess that was the moment I fell in love with you.'

Caitlin caught her breath.

'What did you say?'

'I said, I fell in love with you.'

'You're in love with me?' she whispered.

He nodded and kissed her.

'You know I am.'

Caitlin shook her head.

'But you never said the words,' she murmured. 'And if you don't mind, could you possibly say them again?'

'I'm in love with you, Caitlin Morland,' he said, laughing. 'Is that good enough?'

'For now,' she smiled. 'But I might need reminding at very frequent intervals. Now, shall we take the lovely *Gina* out? You'd better teach me how to drive the thing; I like to keep on top of the competition!'

Ludo laughed and began kissing her again.

And this time Caitlin saw absolutely no need for words.

Also available by Rosie Rushton:

Break Point

Friends, Enemies and Other Tiny Problems

The Secrets of Love

The Leehampton series
Just Don't Make a Scene, Mum!
I Think I'll Just Curl Up and Die!
How Could You Do This to Me, Mum?
Does Anyone Ever Listen?

What a Week series
What a Week Omnibus Books 1 – 3
What a Week Omnibus Books 4 – 6
What a Week to Take a Chance
What a Week to Get Real
What a Week to Risk It All

the Secrets of Love

Rosie Rushton

What would happen if you transferred the traumas of teenage love from Jane Austen's *Sense and Sensibility* to the twenty-first century? How would the Dashwood girls fare without the restraints of nineteenth-century England?

Will Ellie's ever-sensible attitude towards life prevent her from snogging the gorgeous, but somewhat reticent, Blake?

Is Abby's devil-may-care outlook destined to land her in big trouble with Hunter, who specialises in being up himself?

And what about the baby of the family, Georgie? She's a tomboy, with more male friends than anyone, and so strong-willed she'll never take no for an answer!

☆

www.piccadillypress.co.uk

☆ The latest news on forthcoming books

☆ Chapter previews

☆ Author biographies

☆ Fun quizzes

☆ Reader reviews

☆ Competitions and fab prizes

☆ Book features and cool downloads

☆ And much, much more . . .

Log on and check it out!

Piccadilly Press

☆